ILLUSTRATED CLASSIC EDITIONS

Pride and Prejudice

Jane Austen

Adapted by
Fern Seigel

D0804162

Published by Playmore Inc., Publishers and
Waldman Publishing Corp., New York, New York

ILLUSTRATED CLASSIC EDITIONS

Contents

CHAPTER   PAGE

1. A Gentleman Comes to Netherfield 7
2. A Friendly Discussion 17
3. Jane Receives an Invitation 22
4. Darcy and Elizabeth 31
5. The Horrible Mr. Collins 37
6. Mr. Wickham's Appeal 46
7. A Romantic Entanglement 53
8. A Rejected Suitor 64
9. Jane's Heart is Broken 70
10. Off to London 82
11. A Visit to Rosings 89
12. Darcy Pays an Unexpected Call 103
13. An Unusual Courtship 110
14. Love is Revealed 118
15. A Letter of Explanation 127
16. Thinking about the Past 137
17. A Visit to Pemberley 154
18. A Change of Heart 170
19. Scandal! 178
20. Lydia Is Married 188
21. A Dream Fulfilled 197
22. Lady Catherine's Threats 208
23. Happy Endings 223

About the Author

Jane Austen was born in Steventon, Hampshire, England, on December 16, 1775. As was common for women of her class, she was educated at home. At an early age, she began writing sketches and satires of popular novels for her family's entertainment.

As a clergyman's daughter from a well-connected family, she had many opportunities to study the habits of the middle class, the gentry and the aristocracy of late 18th century and early 19th century England.

When she was twenty-one, she began a novel called *First Impressions*, which was an early version of one of her most famous and beloved novels, *Pride and Prejudice*.

In 1801, when her father retired from the ministry, the family moved to the fashionable resort town of Bath. Two years later, Jane Austen sold a first version of *Northanger Abbey* to a London publisher, but the first of her six novels to appear in print was *Sense and Sensibility*. It was published at her own expense in 1811. It was followed by *Pride and Prejudice* (1813), *Mansfield Park* (1814) and *Emma* (1816).

After her father died, in 1805, the family moved again, to Chawton Cottage in Hampshire. Despite this relative retirement, Jane Austen kept in touch with a wider world. She did this mainly through her brothers—one was a rich country gentleman, another a London banker and two were naval officers.

Though her novels were published anonymously, she had many devoted readers, including the Prince Regent and Sir Walter Scott. She wrote her last novel, *Persuasion*, in 1817, the year she died. She is buried in Winchester Cathedral. Jane Austen's identity as an author was announced to the world after her death by her brother Henry.

"My Dear, Have You Heard?"

CHAPTER 1

A Gentleman Comes to Netherfield

It is a fact, everyone agrees, that a young man with money should have a wife. At least, that's the way they thought in England in the nineteenth century. And the Bennet family in Meryton, in Hampshire, certainly agreed! Mrs. Bennet, the mother, was especially concerned that all of her five daughters married well.

"My dear Mr. Bennet, have you heard that Netherfield Park has been rented?" asked Mrs. Bennet. Mr. Bennet, who rarely paid attention to social happenings, had not heard this news.

"Mrs. Long says that Netherfield has been taken by a wealthy young man from the north of England. He is single and his name is Bingley. He possesses a large fortune—four or five thousand pounds a year. What a fine thing it would be if he married one of our girls!" exclaimed Mrs. Bennet.

It became her favorite daydream: Jane, her eldest daughter, would marry the rich Mr. Bingley before the season was over. After all, the business of Mrs. Bennet's life was to get her daughters married!

With that goal in mind, Mr. Bennet went to visit Mr. Bingley. It was the only proper thing to do. In England, it was considered a father's duty to introduce his daughters into good society. So Mr. Bennet paid a social call on Mr. Bingley. He came home in high spirits. His five daughters were to meet the young squire at an upcoming ball!

Mrs. Bennet was delighted! "My girls will

Mr. Bennet Paid a Call on Mr. Bingley.

shine at the dance, Mr. Bennet," she trumpeted. "I just hope that Mr. Bingley will be taken by Jane's beauty and charm." Mrs. Bennet wasn't taking any chances! To make sure he would notice Jane, the Bennets invited him to a small dinner party at Longbourn, their home.

The party was planned carefully–only the finest china and the most delicious foods could be offered to Mr. Bingley. Finally, he arrived, accompanied by a party of four: Mr. Bingley's two sisters, the older sister's husband and Bingley's best friend, a Mr. Darcy.

How excited the Bennets were to meet Mr. Bingley, who was good-looking and gentlemanly. He had a pleasant face and easy manners. But at the dance, his friend, Mr. Darcy, drew everyone's attention. He had a strong personality, handsome features and an income of ten thousand pounds a year!

The gentlemen thought Darcy was a splendid looking man, and the ladies thought he was even better looking than Mr. Bingley. That was until he revealed his bad manners. Mr. Darcy suffered from the sin of pride—and not even a large estate in Derbyshire or a great fortune could make up for that. He was quickly disliked by the Bennets, who found him an unsuitable match for any of their daughters.

Mr. Bingley, in comparison, was elevated in their eyes. Mr. Bingley was a lively young man and eagerly danced every dance. What a contrast between him and his friend!

Mr. Darcy danced only once, with Miss Bingley, and refused to be introduced to any other lady. Instead, he spent the rest of the evening walking about the room. "He has a most deplorable character," declared Mrs. Bennet. Her neighbors agreed. Soon, Mr. Darcy was considered the proudest and most disagreeable man in the world!

"Come, Darcy," said Bingley. "I hate to see you standing about by yourself. It's so much better to dance."

Elizabeth Made Up Her Mind.

"I won't," answered his friend. "You know how I hate to dance unless I know my partner."

"Come on," coaxed Bingley, "there are many pretty girls here this evening."

"You are dancing with the prettiest girl in the room," replied Darcy, looking at Jane Bennet.

"She is the most beautiful girl I ever met! Let me introduce you to one of her sisters, who is also very pretty," Bingley quickly suggested. He indicated Elizabeth Bennet, who was a few feet away.

Darcy turned to look at Elizabeth, caught her eye, then turned away. "She is not pretty enough to tempt me," he said coldly.

"How rude he is!" thought Elizabeth. As Mr. Darcy walked off abruptly, she made up her mind. She would never like Mr. Darcy. Elizabeth was a lively and intelligent young woman. Further, she was very independent and followed her own mind far more than those of the people around her. This was unusual for a girl in that time and place, and Miss Elizabeth Bennet was a most unusual young lady!

Despite Darcy's attitude, the evening passed pleasantly. Bingley's open admiration of Jane put the entire Bennet family in good spirits. Mrs. Bennet may have hated Darcy, but she thought Bingley charming, handsome and elegant. Oh what a match he was for Jane!

When everyone finally left, Jane and Elizabeth were alone in their room, and they talked about the dance. "Mr. Bingley is everything I'd hoped for," admitted Jane, "He's well-bred and funny and has wonderful manners!"

"He is also handsome," Elizabeth teased her sister, "and so he is just perfect!"

Jane and Elizabeth, who besides being sisters were the dearest of friends, spent many happy hours discussing their ideas about love and marriage. Their relationship was like the close friendship between Bingley and Darcy. Darcy valued the easy, open ways of his friend. Bingley valued Darcy's judgment and understanding. But there was a big difference

They Talked About the Dance.

between them: Bingley was liked by everyone; Darcy was always offending people.

The party brought out the differences between the two men. Bingley thought he had never met nicer people or had seen prettier girls. "Jane Bennet is an angel!" he told his friend. Darcy, for his part, saw little to like about the people of Meryton.

"Mrs. Bennet is coarse and unrefined. Your own sisters agree with me," Darcy told Bingley.

"My sisters like Jane Bennet," Bingley replied. "You may think what you like, Darcy, but I don't care about Miss Bennet's mother. I intend to pursue Jane!"

CHAPTER 2

A Friendly Discussion

The next day, Jane, Elizabeth and their friend, Charlotte Lucas, met to discuss the party. The longtime friends talked about Darcy's coldness.

"Miss Bingley told me," said Jane, "that he only speaks to his own friends. With them he is remarkably agreeable."

"Maybe he has an excuse to be proud," suggested Charlotte. "He has family, fortune, everything in his favor."

"Don't Hide Your Feelings," Charlotte warned.

"That is very true," laughed Elizabeth. "Perhaps I could forgive his pride, if he hadn't wounded mine!" Darcy, however, was soon forgotten as the girls soon turned to a more interesting topic—the likelihood of a marriage between Jane and Bingley!

"Don't hide your feelings," Charlotte warned Jane. "Few people can be in love without encouragement. In nine cases out of ten, a woman had better show her affection. Bingley likes you, but you must let him know it."

"Your plan is a good one," noted Elizabeth, "if the object is to get just any husband. But Jane wants someone extra special. She wants to be happy with her choice."

"Happiness in marriage is entirely a matter of chance," Charlotte insisted.

Even as Elizabeth discussed the ways of love, she never guessed that she had become of interest to Mr. Darcy! At first, he told his friends that she held no attractions for him. But no sooner had he said this than he began to notice her good features. Her beautiful eyes. Her intelligent expression. And he was charmed by her playful manners.

Elizabeth, however, had not the slightest idea of how Darcy felt. He decided to make his feelings, in some way, known to her. The next time he saw her, at Sir William Lucas' party, he quickly asked her to dance. But Elizabeth declined his invitation. Remembering his rudeness at their last meeting, she turned away. Yet instead of being offended, Darcy was intrigued. But he couldn't understand or explain this sudden new feeling, not even to himself!

Elizabeth Declined His Invitation.

CHAPTER 3

Jane Receives an Invitation

Marriage and money were the main subjects on Mrs. Bennet's mind. Jane and Elizabeth talked about love. The next sister, Mary, was studious and uninterested in romance. But Kitty and Lydia, the youngest and most empty-headed of the Bennet girls, were already flirting with soldiers at the regiment that was stationed nearby.

Of course, marriage was not a subject to consider lightly. Mr. Bennet's income was only two thousands pounds a year. Unfortunately for his daughters, his property would go to a distant male cousin. And so, money was forever on Mrs. Bennet's mind.

"If a nice young colonel, with five or six thousand pounds a year, should want one of my girls, I shall heartily approve," Mrs. Bennet often exclaimed, both to herself and to Mr. Bennet, whenever that patient gentleman gave her the chance.

She was interrupted this time by a servant who brought a letter from Netherfield for Jane.

"Miss Bingley," said Jane breathlessly, "has invited me to dinner." Mrs. Bennet was thrilled. A horse was immediately brought round to the house. Mr. Bennet worried about the bad weather, but his wife would not hear of any delay.

"This is a wonderful sign, dear," she exclaimed. "Use your charm to make a good impression." So, in spite of the rain and cold, Jane rode the four miles to Netherfield. The

"I Will Go at Once!"

next morning, however, brought the family disturbing news. A note arrived from Jane, explaining that she had a bad cold and fever. The doctor who had been summoned suggested she spend a few days at Netherfield until she got better.

Mrs. Bennet was thrilled by the unexpected event. "This will give young Bingley and Jane a chance to see more of each other!" she said happily.

"I'm worried about Jane! How do we know if she's all right? I will go to Netherfield at once!" Elizabeth said.

"I have no horses to spare, Lizzy," said her father.

"No matter," said his determined daughter, "I shall walk to Netherfield."

On her arrival, Elizabeth was shown into the breakfast parlor. Mr. Darcy said very little, but thought to himself how pretty she looked after her long walk. Then Elizabeth was immediately taken to Jane, who was almost too ill to speak to her sister.

They had a long visit, and Elizabeth felt she should go, but Jane wanted her to stay. The Bingleys, not wanting to alarm Jane, in her serious condition, agreed. A servant was sent to inform the Bennets that both girls were staying at Netherfield until further notice.

That night at dinner, Jane's condition was explained to Bingley. His concern for Jane was evident. At the same time, he was most kind to Elizabeth, who thought him an ideal match for her beloved sister. After dinner, Elizabeth excused herself and went to Jane's room.

"Jane Bennet is a very sweet girl, and I wish her well with all my heart," Miss Bingley sighed, once Elizabeth was out of earshot. "But with such low family connections, I am afraid there is little chance for her."

"It doesn't make the girls one jot less wonderful," cried Bingley, in the Bennet sisters' defense.

"But it must lessen their chance of marrying

His Concern for Jane Was Evident.

men of consideration in the world," said Darcy.

To this, Bingley made no answer. Some time later, Elizabeth rejoined them. The rest of the party decided to play whist, a card game. Elizabeth, too worried about her sister to concentrate, declined the invitation politely. Miss Bingley, who was catty, rather than friendly, seized the opportunity to tease Elizabeth.

"Miss Eliza Bennet," said Miss Bingley, "despises cards. She is a great reader and has no pleasure in anything else."

"I have pleasure in *many* things," replied Elizabeth.

Darcy, sensing a challenge, turned the conversation to the subject of accomplished women. "I know only six women who are really accomplished," he said. "I think such a woman must have appreciation of the arts, speak several languages and be knowledgeable about books," he said.

"I am not surprised at your knowing only six such women," Elizabeth said. "I am amazed that you know any!"

Darcy looked at her very carefully. It was not the answer he had expected from her. Beneath Elizabeth Bennet's laughing exterior, there was a very thoughtful young woman indeed. She had, it seemed, a great deal of wit, and intelligence. That was not the sort of thing he would think to be among the traits of a girl who lived quietly and simply in the country.

Perhaps he had been too quick to judge Miss Bennet. Perhaps his pride had gotten in the way once again!

Mrs. Bennet Was Summoned.

CHAPTER 4

Darcy and Elizabeth

The next morning, Mrs. Bennet was summoned to Netherfield. Jane was still very ill and it was decided that she should not return home in her present state. Satisfied that the illness was not dangerous, Mrs. Bennet had no wish to take her away from Netherfield.

"I am sure," she said, "if it was not for such good friends I do not know what would have become of her. She has the sweetest disposition. I tell my other girls that they are nothing compared to *her.*"

Mrs. Bennet repeated her thanks to Mr. Bingley for his many kindnesses to Jane. Lydia, who had accompanied her mother to Netherfield, reminded Bingley of his promise to hold a ball. "Once Jane is well enough to attend, I will see to the ball personally," he promised. Delighted with his good spirits and the promise of Jane's recovery, Mrs. Bennet and Lydia soon left.

Elizabeth returned to Jane's room. Once she was gone, the two Bingley sisters resumed their gossip. This time, however, Darcy refused to listen to any criticism of Elizabeth Bennet.

Was he falling in love with her? he asked himself.

He wasn't the only one who noticed the change in the air. That evening, Elizabeth sensed how often Mr. Darcy's eyes followed her. She couldn't imagine why, since she thought that he quite disliked her.

"Would you care to dance a reel?" he asked

"Once Jane Is Well Enough."

all of sudden.

"I know you want me to say 'Yes,' so you could criticize my taste in music, but I delight in overthrowing those kind of schemes. I do not want to dance a reel," she cried. "So hate me if you dare!"

"I do not dare," said Darcy politely.

Elizabeth was amazed at his gallantry, since she had so clearly snubbed him. Darcy did not care. He had never before been so bewitched by any woman.

Jane was soon well enough to join the others downstairs. Bingley was full of joy and attentive to her every want and need. Elizabeth saw it all with great delight. Darcy saw only Elizabeth, and anxious to speak with her alone, engaged her in a lively conversation about pride and temperament.

"I cannot forget the faults of others as quickly as I should," he admitted. "My good opinion, once lost, is lost for ever."

"*That* is a fault!" cried Elizabeth. "I cannot

laugh at you. You are in no danger from me."

"No one is perfect. There is in everyone some particular character flaw," he baited her.

"If so, I'd say that your particular defect is a desire to hate everybody," Elizabeth said lightly.

"And yours," he replied with a smile, "is to misunderstand them."

Elizabeth laughed and rejoined the others.

Darcy, after a few moments, thought he might be in another kind of danger—paying Elizabeth too much attention!

"You Have Been Extremely Kind."

CHAPTER 5

The Horrible Mr. Collins

The next morning, the sisters agreed that Jane was well enough to leave Netherfield and Elizabeth wrote to tell her mother. Mrs. Bennet would have preferred them to remain at Netherfield for the following week. But Elizabeth was determined and urged Jane to borrow Mr. Bingley's carriage immediately.

Bingley greeted this request with genuine regret, but Jane stood her ground. "You have been extremely kind to me and I thank your sisters. But I am better now and it is time for me to return home."

To Mr. Darcy, it was welcome news. Elizabeth had been at Netherfield long enough. He was becoming too attracted to her. To discourage her from thinking he would pay her any more attention, he did not bother to say goodbye. On Sunday, after church, the Bennet girls returned to Longbourn.

"I hope, my dear," said Mr. Bennet to his wife at breakfast the following morning, "that you ordered a lot for dinner, because I expect an additional guest."

"Who do you mean?" she asked.

"It is my cousin, Mr. Collins. The man who will inherit my money and this house when I die."

"Don't talk to me of that horrible man," cried his wife. "It is the cruelest thing in the world that your estate should be taken away from your children."

"Mr. Collins sent me a letter," explained Mr.

" . . . That Horrible Man."

Bennet. "He has been ordained a minister and in the parish of the Honorable Lady Catherine de Bourgh. He feels badly about the inheritance. In fact, he says it is his duty to promote peace. At four o'clock, therefore, we may expect this peacemaking gentleman," said Mr. Bennet, as he folded up the letter.

The Bennet family was divided as to this relative of theirs. Mrs. Bennet was anxious that Mr. Collins be convinced to make amends, Elizabeth thought him likely to be odd, and her father always found him to be a strange mixture of humbleness and self-importance. All the family were interested in meeting him.

Mr. Collins was on time and was greeted with great politeness. He was an overweight man of twenty-five, with a puffed-up air and stiff manners. He complimented the Bennets on their beautiful daughters and slyly hinted at a marriage to one of them!

During dinner, Mr. Bennet asked about Mr. Collins' patroness, Lady Catherine de Bourgh.

Mr. Collins was full of her praises.

"Lady Catherine is all one could wish for in a person of importance. Such manners! Such style! She advises me to marry as soon as possible."

Elizabeth and Jane exchanged secret smiles. What a funny man!

"You possess the talent of flattery," observed Mr. Bennet, who found his cousin as absurd as he remembered.

But it was not poor Mr. Collins' fault. He was just not a sensible man. As a boy, he had been wrongly taught that flattery was the answer to ignorance and fear, both of which traits he had much of.

As such, he was a source of comedy to the Bennet girls. They hated how he worshipped Lady Catherine. They preferred more independent, honest men.

Still, Mr. Collins could boast of a good house and income, and, as such, he was considered a good catch, certainly by himself! And he did

A Walk into Meryton

feel badly about the estate and had hopes of being friends with the Bennets. But his solution was to marry one of the daughters! In this way, he thought, he could make up to them for inheriting their father's estate. He didn't realize how ridiculous his mannerisms made him to Elizabeth and Jane, at least.

Moreover, Collins thought them all lovely. In order to get to know them better, he suggested they take a walk into their little town of Meryton. But there the attention of the ladies was soon caught by another young man, whom they had never seen before. Their friend Mr. Denny introduced his friend, Mr. Wickham, who was an officer in the army. The Bennet girls were quite taken with Mr. Wickham, who was dashing and pleasant.

They hadn't spoken to Wickham long when they saw Darcy and Bingley riding down the street. Elizabeth noticed Wickham and Darcy look at each other with astonishment. Both men flushed. Then they set off. Was there trouble between Wickham and Darcy, she wondered.

The other Bennet girls were too busy with Mr. Denny and Mr. Wickham to notice. The soldiers escorted the young ladies to the door of their uncle's house and accepted an invitation to stay for dinner. Although every woman who was present noticed Mr. Wickham, he chose to sit next to Elizabeth. They quickly fell into easy conversation.

With such a rival for the ladies' attention as Mr. Wickham, poor Mr. Collins seemed to disappear from view!

The Other Bennet Girls Were Too Busy.

CHAPTER 6

Mr. Wickham's Appeal

While the rest of the party sat down to play cards, Wickham and Elizabeth talked. She was very eager to learn of his acquaintance with Mr. Darcy.

"I take it Netherfield is not far from Meryton. Has Mr. Darcy been staying there?" Mr. Wickham asked.

"About a month," replied Elizabeth. "He is a man of very large property in Derbyshire, I understand."

"Yes," replied Wickham, "his estate is a noble one. I have been connected with his family from my infancy."

Elizabeth was stunned by this news. "I find him very disagreeable," she said. "He is not at all liked here. Everybody is disgusted with his pride."

"I cannot pretend to be sorry," said Wickham. "The world is blinded by his fortune and importance, or frightened by his high and demanding manners."

"I hope your plans won't be affected by his being here," Elizabeth said.

"Oh no, it is not for *me* to be driven away by Mr. Darcy. If *he* wishes to avoid seeing *me*, he must go. We are not on friendly terms, and it always gives me pain to meet him," Wickham said. Then he explained his reason.

"I was not meant for a military life. The church ought to have been my profession. I was brought up for the church, and I should now have a most valuable place, had it not been for

"This Is Quite Shocking!"

Darcy," he said.

"His father, the late Mr. Darcy, bequeathed me the best parish in his power. He was my godfather, and he was always very kind to me. He meant to provide for me, but when the position became available, it was given to another."

"Good heavens!" cried Elizabeth. "Why didn't you get a lawyer?"

"It was an informal bequest. A man of honor could not have doubted the intention, but Mr. Darcy chose to doubt it," Wickham shrugged.

"This is quite shocking! He deserves to be publicly disgraced," announced Elizabeth angrily.

"Some time or other he will be. But not by me. I cannot forget his father, so I can never defy or expose his son."

Elizabeth honored him for such feelings, and thought Wickham more handsome than ever. "But what," she said after a pause, "can his motive have been?"

"I think his father's attachment to me must

have irritated him. He hated the competition we were in, the preference paid to me," explained Wickham.

"I did not suspect him of such revenge, such injustice as this!" cried Elizabeth. After a few minutes reflection, however, she continued, "It's no wonder that Mr. Darcy's pride has made him unjust to you!"

"He does have pride," agreed Wickham. "Family pride, brotherly pride."

"What sort of a girl is Miss Darcy?" Elizabeth inquired.

"I wish I could call her pleasant. But she is too much like her brother. Very proud. As a child, she was affectionate," Wickham said fondly. "She is now a lovely girl of sixteen. She lives with a lady in London who supervises her education."

Mr. Wickham's attention was diverted by Mr. Collins for a few moments. Then he turned and asked Elizabeth whether her cousin was acquainted with the family of de Bourgh.

Diverted by Mr. Collins

"Lady Catherine de Bourgh," she replied, "is his patroness. She has recently given him a parish."

"You do know that Lady Catherine de Bourgh and Lady Anne Darcy were sisters. She is Mr. Darcy's aunt," said Wickham.

I never heard of her existence till yesterday," replied Elizabeth.

"Her daughter, Miss de Bourgh, will inherit a very large fortune. It is believed that she and Darcy will marry and join the two estates one day," said Wickham knowingly.

This information made Elizabeth smile. Poor Miss Bingley's eager attempts to Darcy were all in vain. Elizabeth then bade Mr. Wickham goodbye. Once she left, she could think of nothing else but him!

CHAPTER 7

A Romantic Entanglement

The next day Elizabeth told Jane what had passed between Mr. Wickham and herself. Jane listened with astonishment and concern. Could Darcy be so unworthy of Mr. Bingley's friendship? Yet, it was not in her nature to question the truthfulness of someone who seemed as nice as Wickham did.

"Can Mr. Darcy's closest friends be so deceived by him?" Jane wondered.

"I can believe Mr. Bingley's being ignorant of

Jane Listened with Astonishment.

the facts," replied her sister. "But why would Mr. Wickham make up such a story? If it's untrue, let Mr. Darcy contradict it."

"I don't know what to think," said a distressed Jane.

"I know exactly what to think," replied a determined Elizabeth.

The two young ladies were interrupted by the arrival of Mr. Bingley and his sisters. They came with their personal invitation to the long-expected ball at Netherfield. The idea of the Netherfield ball was eagerly anticipated by every Bennet girl, who dreamed of romance and dashing young gentlemen!

Jane pictured to herself a happy evening in the company of Mr. Bingley, while Elizabeth thought of dancing with Mr. Wickham. Not only were the girls invited, even Mr. Collins was included in the Bingleys' hospitality. He immediately asked Elizabeth for the first two dances.

Elizabeth was caught off-guard. She had

expected to share these dances with Wickham. Still, Mr. Collins' offer was accepted with as much grace as a disappointed girl could muster. Then it hit her. He meant to propose to her! She had noticed his increasing friendliness to her, and even her mother thought Mr. Collins a good match. Elizabeth, however, pretended not to take the hint.

Until Elizabeth entered the drawing-room at Netherfield and looked in vain for Mr. Wickham, she never doubted he'd be there. Had he been purposely not invited by the Bingleys' on Mr. Darcy's behalf? Elizabeth was very suspicious.

In his absence, Elizabeth had to keep her promise to dance with Mr. Collins. He was awkward and a terrible dancing partner. Elizabeth's poor feet were the proof!

She danced next with an officer; then, before she could catch her breath, Mr. Darcy took her by the hand and led her onto the dance floor. For the longest time, they didn't speak.

A Terrible Dancing Partner

"It is your turn to say something, Mr. Darcy," Elizabeth exclaimed, after commenting on the music.

"Do you always talk while you're dancing?" he asked.

"Sometimes. It would look odd to be entirely silent," she answered.

So he asked her if she and her sisters often walked into Meryton. She said yes, then added, "When you met us there, we had just made a new acquaintance."

The effect of her words was immediate. A deep shade of red spread over his face, but he said nothing. Finally he spoke. "Mr. Wickham is blessed with such manners that ensure he makes friends. I'm not as convinced, however, that he can keep them."

"Well," Elizabeth retorted, "he's lost your friendship and he'll suffer for it all his life!"

Darcy did not reply to her accusation. He quickly changed the subject to books.

But Elizabeth was not to be ignored. "I

remember you once told me that you hardly ever forgave anyone. You must be very careful in your judgments then."

"I am," he said in a firm voice.

"And are you never blinded by prejudice?" Elizabeth asked pointedly.

"I hope not. May I ask why all the questions?"

"I'm just trying to decide the kind of man you are," she said, as they separated. Elizabeth was unmoved by their discussion, but Darcy felt himself overpowered by his feelings for her.

They had parted only a moment when Miss Bingley came toward Elizabeth with a nasty look on her face. "I hear you are taken with George Wickham! Did he tell you he was the son of the late Mr. Darcy's butler? He claims young Mr. Darcy treated him badly. This is untrue. I don't know the particulars, but I know Mr. Darcy is not to blame for any such treatment."

"According to you, his guilt and his birth are

Miss Bingley Turned Away with a Sneer.

the same thing," said Elizabeth angrily. "I have heard nothing worse than his being the son of a butler and he told me that himself. You mistake me if you expect to influence me with such an attack. I see nothing in it but your ignorance and Mr. Darcy's malice!"

Miss Bingley turned away with a sneer, and Elizabeth was soon joined by Jane.

"Mr. Bingley does not know the whole story between Wickham and Darcy, but he will vouch for the good conduct of his friend," said Jane. "He believes that Wickham is not a respectable man."

"Mr. Bingley does not know Wickham himself?" asked Elizabeth.

"No," said Jane.

"Then the account he has received is from Mr. Darcy. Mr. Bingley's defense of his friend is admirable, but he is not a reliable source if he has no firsthand information," cautioned Elizabeth.

The sisters discussed happier matters, such

as Jane's delight in Bingley's attentiveness. Elizabeth could see that the two had a deep love for one another. Jane could enjoy all the blessings of a marriage of true love.

Elizabeth wasn't alone in her sentiments, her mother could talk of nothing else! Elizabeth tried to stop her mother from boasting of Jane's future possibilities in public, but her effort was hopeless.

Mrs. Bennet was a vain and silly woman who often embarrassed her daughters. Not surprisingly, Mrs. Bennet returned to Longbourn in high spirits, convinced that her favorite child Jane would soon be settled in Netherfield and poor Elizabeth would eventually marry silly Mr. Collins!

Her Mother Could Talk of Nothing Else!

CHAPTER 8

A Rejected Suitor

Indeed, the very next day, Mr. Collins asked Mrs. Bennet if he could be alone with Elizabeth. They met in the drawing room and he immediately stated his intentions. "As soon as I entered this house, I singled you out as my future wife," he began.

"I should state my reasons for coming to Hampshire. One, I think it right that all clergymen marry to set a good example. Two, I think it will add to my happiness, and three, because my patroness wishes it. Of course, I could have searched for a wife in my own parish," he added, "but I feel I owe it to your family to make my inheritance easier by marrying one of its daughters."

"Thank you for the compliment you pay me," Elizabeth began, "but I must say no."

"It is not usual for young ladies to reject a man they secretly wish to accept," he said smugly.

"Mr. Collins! I am perfectly serious," Elizabeth cried. "You could not make me happy, and I am the last woman in the world who could make you happy. You have satisfied your feelings toward my family, but I consider this matter settled."

"You are charming!" he responded, trying to be gallant. "I'm sure you will eventually accept my proposal."

Elizabeth walked out of the room. When she said something, she meant it. Anyone who did not understand that, certainly did not

"An Unhappy Alternative, Elizabeth."

understand her! If he would not believe her refusal, perhaps he would believe the negative answer her father was sure to give him!

Mr. Collins lost no time in telling Mrs. Bennet of her daughter's refusal. Her mother was so angry she summoned Elizabeth to the library to speak to her father. Mrs. Bennet felt sure her husband would talk some sense into Elizabeth.

"Your mother insists upon your accepting his hand. Is this not so, Mrs. Bennet?" Mr. Bennet asked.

"Yes, or I will never see her again," his wife exclaimed.

"An unhappy alternative is before you, Elizabeth," said her father. "From this day you must be a stranger to one of your parents. Your mother will never see you again if you do not marry Mr. Collins, and I will never see you again if you do!" He smiled at his daughter.

Elizabeth could not but smile back at her father's words, but Mrs. Bennet, who expected a different reaction from her husband, was very disappointed. In addition, Mrs. Bennet was furious at her daughter's independent behavior.

In the midst of this family turmoil, Charlotte Lucas came to spend the day. She was met in the vestibule by Lydia, who, flying to her, cried in a half-whisper, "Guess what happened? Mr. Collins proposed to Lizzy, and she turned him down!"

Charlotte's reply was blocked by the entrance of Jane and Elizabeth.

They spoke for a few minutes. Mrs. Bennet bemoaned the curse of undutiful children and Mr. Collins finally accepted the inevitable refusal. From this moment on, he decided to ignore Elizabeth, thinking he would punish her this way.

But Elizabeth was happy and relieved to be rid of the unwanted, boring attention of this silly man.

"Guess What Happened?"

CHAPTER 9

Jane's Heart is Broken

After a silent breakfast, Elizabeth and the younger girls walked to Meryton to see Mr. Wickham. Elizabeth was pleased to see him. "Why did you not attend the ball?" she asked. "I think you would have enjoyed it."

He explained to Elizabeth that he had voluntarily decided to avoid the ball at Netherfield, so as not to cause problems for Mr. Darcy. His sensitivity increased her affectionate feelings for him.

Soon after they returned home from town, Elizabeth looked for Jane. She wanted to see her sister alone, and to tell her all the news of Wickham, but it wasn't to be. Jane was too upset. "Jane, whatever is the matter?" asked Elizabeth anxiously.

"I have received a letter from Caroline Bingley. It says that the Bingleys have left Netherfield and are on their way to London. They have no plans to be here at present. It is evident that he won't return this winter," Jane sighed sadly. "I don't understand why he is doing this. There is more," she added. "Caroline writes that Georgiana Darcy is a most accomplished young lady. She hopes that Bingley will marry her!"

"I have a different opinion," stated Elizabeth. "I think Miss Bingley knows that her brother is in love with you, but *she* wants him to marry Miss Darcy. She hopes that by keeping him in London she will convince him to forget all about you."

Mr. Collins Still Moped Around.

"Oh, Jane. We are not rich enough or grand enough for Miss Bingley. Caroline thinks if her brother marries Darcy's sister then she may have a chance to marry Darcy herself! Her plan might even succeed if Miss de Bourgh were out of the way. But don't worry, Jane, no one can alter his love for you," Elizabeth consoled her sister.

While Jane pined over Bingley, Mr. Collins still moped around. Elizabeth was very grateful for the presence of her friend Charlotte, who always engaged him in conversation. Charlotte's kindness, however, had another motive: She wanted to marry Mr. Collins herself! Charlotte's persistence was quickly rewarded. Just days after being rejected by Elizabeth, Mr. Collins had proposed to Charlotte. And Charlotte, whose only desire was for a house of her own, was happy to accept.

Sir William and Lady Lucas, her parents, were delighted with the match. Since they had no money to leave her, Mr. Collins' position made him a most eligible match for their daughter. Lady Lucas even began calculating how many more years Mr. Bennet was likely to live. After all, one day the Longbourn estate would belong to Mr. Collins!

Charlotte was more than satisfied. She knew that Mr. Collins wasn't a serious man and that his company was rather annoying. But this marriage would give her a position in life that was satisfactory enough for her. Charlotte was content.

Jane and Elizabeth, meanwhile, had little time for Charlotte or Mr. Collins. They were more concerned about Bingley's sudden departure. It was rumored that he would not return to Netherfield for Christmas, a report that angered Mrs. Bennet, and which she insisted was a scandalous lie.

Even Elizabeth began to fear for Jane's happiness. She worried that Bingley's sisters would keep him away. The united efforts of his two unfeeling sisters and Darcy, his best

Concerned About Bingley

friend, assisted by the attractions of Miss Darcy, might be enough for him to forget Jane.

As for Jane, her anxiety was even more painful than Elizabeth's, but she hid her true feelings. Still, an hour seldom passed in which Mrs. Bennet did not talk of Bingley, or remind Jane that she had been treated badly. It needed all of Jane's patience to bear her mother's harsh words.

In fairness, Mrs. Bennett was really in a most pitiful state. The very mention of Bingley threw her into despair, and she heard talk of him wherever she went. Moreover, the sight of Charlotte Lucas was oppressive to her. As her likely replacement in the Longbourn house, she regarded Charlotte with jealous hatred. She complained bitterly to her husband.

"My dear, do not give way to such gloomy thoughts," he comforted her. "Let us hope for better things. Maybe I will survive you." This gentle irony did not console Mrs. Bennet, who left the room to avoid her husband's remarks.

The inheritance preoccupied Mrs. Bennet, but not her daughters. They were too busy thinking of their own lives and what their futures might hold. Jane's situation was the most upsetting. "Will he return to Hertfordshire as he promised me?" she asked herself. "Or have I lost him forever?"

When Miss Bingley's next letter arrived, it put an end to Jane's doubts. The very first sentence explained that they were settled in London for the winter. Hope was gone. Caroline even had the gall to boast of her brother's affection for Miss Darcy!

Elizabeth heard this and fumed. Her heart was divided between concern for her sister, and resentment against the others. That Bingley was really fond of Jane, she never doubted. As much as she liked him, she could not think of him without anger. Why was he such a slave to his sister and friends? Why had he sacrificed his happiness with Jane? Jane refused to blame Bingley, but Elizabeth did.

"Can Charlotte Be in Her Right Mind?"

"There seems to be a shortage of merit and sense in some people. I can cite two recent examples: Bingley's departure and Charlotte's marriage," she noted. "Mr. Collins is a conceited, narrow-minded fool! No self-respecting woman would ever marry such a man. Can Charlotte be in her right mind?"

"You mentioned two instances, Lizzy," said Jane. "I don't blame Bingley. We must not expect a young man to always act responsibly. My vanity deceived me. Women think admiration means more than it does."

"And men make us think that it does!" Elizabeth cried.

"Do you think his sisters influence him?" asked Jane. "I'm sure they only wish for his happiness."

"They may wish many things besides his happiness," countered Elizabeth. "They may wish he increases his wealth, so they may wish him to marry a rich girl."

"If they believed he loved me, they would not

try to part us," said Jane. "If he loved me, they could not succeed. This kind of talk upsets me. I can't take much more."

Elizabeth respected Jane's wishes. From then on, they rarely mentioned Bingley's name.

They Rarely Mentioned Bingley's Name.

CHAPTER 10

Off to London

Mr. Wickham's presence helped dispel the gloom at Longbourn. Darcy's mistreatment of him was openly believed, and Darcy was thought to be the worst of men.

On the following Monday, Mrs. Bennet's brother and his wife came to spend Christmas at Longbourn. Mr. Gardiner was a kind gentleman. Mrs. Gardiner was a great favorite with all her nieces.

After distributing her gifts, Mrs. Gardiner

asked Elizabeth privately about Jane and Bingley. "I never saw a more adoring suitor. He was totally in love with her," Elizabeth replied.

"Do you think we could persuade her to return with us to London? A change of scene might do her good," said her aunt. "We live in a different part of town. Our social circles are so different, it's unlikely she and Bingley would meet."

The Gardiners stayed a week at Longbourn, and what with them, the neighbors, the Lucases and the officers, there were parties every day. When the party was at home, Wickham always attended. On these occasions, Mrs. Gardiner carefully watched Elizabeth and Wickham together. Without supposing them to be in love, their closeness made her uneasy. Was he really good for Elizabeth, she wondered.

Mrs. Gardiner decided to approach her niece the very next day. "You are too sensible a girl, Lizzy, to fall in love merely because you are

Without Even a Goodbye

warned against it. So be on your guard. I have nothing to say against him," she hastened to add. "He is an interesting young man; if he had money, all would be well. But as it is, you must not let your fancy run away with you. You have sense, and we all expect you to use it."

"My dear aunt, I am not in love with Mr. Wickham. I can promise you that I won't rush into anything. I will try to do what I think best." Elizabeth thanked her aunt for her concern, and they parted on good terms. The Gardiners left the next day, with Jane in tow.

Once in London, Jane wrote to Caroline Bingley, hoping that they could meet. Four weeks went by without a word. One day, Caroline paid Jane a surprise visit.

"I can't stay long, Jane. Bingley does not intend to ever return to Netherfield. I know that you care for my brother, and I thought you should know the truth," Miss Bingley said and then, without even a goodbye, she rushed off.

Jane was terribly shaken. She wrote immediately to tell Elizabeth the sad news. This letter gave Elizabeth much pain. The situation with Bingley was hopeless. Poor Jane!

About this time, Mrs. Gardiner paid a brief visit to Elizabeth. She reminded her niece of her warning concerning Wickham. The news Elizabeth told her pleased her aunt more than herself. The week before, Wickham wrote that he was now attached to another woman. The new lady's charms consisted of a fortune of ten thousand pounds and Wickham was courting her with all his heart.

"But Elizabeth," her aunt mused, "What sort of girl is this? I'm sorry to think Wickham so money hungry."

Elizabeth was exhausted by all the talk of romance and money and longed for a diversion. So she decided to visit her friend Charlotte and her new husband, Mr. Collins. A journey was planned. Elizabeth would accompany Sir William and his second daughter, Maria, to Hunsford, where Charlotte now lived.

She Decided to Visit Her Friend.

Although Mr. Collins was far from being a favorite of Elizabeth's, she was eager to see Charlotte, and a change of scenery, after all, was supposed to be a remedy for so many problems. It was with a hopeful heart that Elizabeth packed her small trunks and got ready for her new adventure.

CHAPTER 11

A Visit to Rosings

Every part of the trip was new and interesting to Elizabeth, and she was in good spirits. She was looking forward to her visit to Hunsford. The journey went swiftly and soon she could see the parsonage—the gardens and the house and the church.

Mr. and Mrs. Collins appeared at the door, as the carriage stopped at their small gate. Charlotte welcomed her friend warmly and Elizabeth was glad she had come. But she saw

Collins Was Besides Himself with Joy.

instantly that marriage had not changed Mr. Collins.

Indeed, when he said anything that might embarrass his wife, which was often, Charlotte would blush, yet pretend not to notice. When Mr. Collins was elsewhere, the house had a more comfortable air about it. Elizabeth knew that Lady Catherine was at her own home at Rosings, and Mr. Collins was eager to inform everyone present of the magnificence of his patroness.

"We dine at Rosings twice every week," he boasted, "and are never allowed to walk home. Her carriage is regularly ordered for us. I'm pleased to say she has invited all of us to Rosings for dinner tomorrow."

Mr. Collins was besides himself with joy at Lady Catherine's invitation. The chance to display the grandeur of his patroness to his visitors was exactly what he had wished for. The great hour finally arrived. They were led into the ante-chamber of the Rosings dining room and introduced.

Lady Catherine was a tall, large woman, with strong features. She had a commanding air and spoke with great authority. She intimidated the others, but Elizabeth found her exactly as Wickham had described. Miss de Bourgh, her daughter, was pale and sickly and spoke little to their guests.

The dinner itself was exceedingly well done. There were all the servants and all the elegant food which Mr. Collins had promised. He took his seat at the bottom of the table. He carved and ate and praised Lady Catherine endlessly.

"You esteem us by this most beautiful table," he purred. "Each delicacy is a treat for us."

Elizabeth groaned inwardly. What a toady he was! How lucky she was to have escaped Charlotte's fate. But she kept her thoughts to herself, and smiled and spoke to everyone, expressing her happiness at being there.

When the meal was over, the ladies returned to the drawing room. There, Lady Catherine

Lady Catherine Spoke with Great Authority.

dominated all the conversation. She gave her opinion on every subject; clearly, she was not used to having her judgment questioned. "Are any of your younger sisters out in society, Miss Bennet?" Lady Catherine inquired of Elizabeth.

"Yes, ma'am, all."

"All five out at once? Very odd! The younger ones out before the elders are married! Your younger sisters must be very young?"

"My youngest is not sixteen. But I believe the last born has as much a right to pleasure as the first," Elizabeth answered.

"Upon my word," said her ladyship, "you give your opinions very decidedly for a young person! How old are you?"

"With three younger sisters grown up," replied Elizabeth smiling, "you can't expect me to answer that question."

Lady Catherine seemed quite astonished at not receiving a direct answer. Elizabeth suspected she was the first person who had ever defied that lady!

The gentlemen soon joined them. The tea trays were cleared and card tables were set up. When Lady Catherine and her daughter had played for as long as they wanted, the evening was over, and the carriage brought around. As soon as they had driven off, Mr. Collins asked Elizabeth her opinion of Rosings. For Charlotte's sake, she made her reply more favorable than it really was.

In truth, Rosings didn't impress Elizabeth, but she was enjoying her visit. She dined at Rosings twice a week. She took walks in the grove daily. Easter was approaching and Elizabeth heard that Mr. Darcy was expected to visit his aunt shortly. In fact, the very next week, Mr. Darcy and his cousin, Colonel Fitzwilliam, arrived at her door!

Colonel Fitzwilliam was about thirty, not handsome, but a very polite, agreeable gentleman. Mr. Darcy looked the same, with his usual reserve. Elizabeth merely curtseyed to

She Spoke More to Darcy.

him, without saying a word.

Over the course of the next few weeks, Elizabeth had ample time to study both men. Colonel Fitzwilliam's manners were much admired at the parsonage, and the ladies felt he added greatly to the delights of their visit. It was some days, however, before they received another invitation.

At the proper hour, they joined the party in Lady Catherine's drawing room. Her ladyship received them politely enough, but it was plain that their presence was considered second best. She was taken entirely by her nephews. She spoke to Darcy more than to any other person in the room.

Colonel Fitzwilliam talked of travel, new books and music. Elizabeth found him extremely entertaining. They talked with such spirit that both Lady Catherine and Darcy noticed. He always seemed to be watching her, Elizabeth thought.

When coffee was over, Colonel Fitzwilliam

reminded Elizabeth that she had promised to play the piano for him. He drew a chair near her. Darcy also stationed himself in front of Elizabeth, who suddenly turned to him.

"You mean to frighten me, Mr. Darcy," she said with a smile. "But my courage always rises with every attempt to intimidate me."

"I've known you long enough to know you find great enjoyment in professing opinions which are not your own," he said.

Elizabeth laughed heartily at this picture of herself. "Mr. Darcy, it is very dangerous of you to say this. You are provoking me to answer back, and I may say something that would shock your relatives."

"I am not afraid of you," he said, smilingly.

"I should like to hear how he behaves among strangers," grinned Colonel Fitzwilliam, his cousin.

"You shall hear then," Elizabeth promised, "but prepare yourself for something very dreadful. The first time I saw him was at a

She Promised to Play.

ball. He danced only four dances, though there were few gentlemen. Women were forced to stay seated, because they had no partners. Mr. Darcy, you cannot deny this."

"I had not at that time the honor of knowing any lady there beyond my own party," he explained.

"True, but can nobody be introduced in a ballroom?" Elizabeth charged.

"Perhaps," lamented Darcy, "I should have judged better. But I am uncomfortable talking to strangers."

"Shall we ask your cousin why a man of sense and education is uncomfortable introducing himself to strangers?" Elizabeth asked the colonel with a smile.

"It is because he will not trouble himself," replied Fitzwilliam only half-teasingly.

"I certainly have not the talent which some people possess," said Darcy, "of conversing easily with people I have never seen before."

"My fingers," said Elizabeth, "do not move

easily over the piano keys the way some women's do. But that's my own fault—I don't bother to practice."

Darcy smiled, and said, "You are perfectly right. Neither of us perform for strangers."

Here they were interrupted by Lady Catherine, who insisted on knowing what they were talking about. Smiling to herself, Elizabeth immediately began playing again until her ladyship's carriage was ready to take them back to Charlotte's house.

Darcy Entered the Room.

CHAPTER 12

Darcy Pays an Unexpected Call

Elizabeth was sitting by herself the next morning and writing to Jane when she was startled by a ring at the door. Her friends had gone shopping in town, and she wasn't expecting any visitors. To her very great surprise, Mr. Darcy entered the room. He seemed astonished to find her alone, and quickly apologized for his intrusion.

They sat down, and after her polite inquiries of everyone at Rosings were made, they lapsed into total silence. It was absolutely necessary to think of something, anything, to say.

"How suddenly you all quit Netherfield last November, Mr. Darcy! Mr. Bingley and his sisters were well, I hope, when you left London," Elizabeth murmured.

"Perfectly so. I thank you," he replied courteously.

"I understood that Mr. Bingley has no interest in returning to Netherfield again?" she asked.

"I have never heard him say so, but it's probably the case. He has many friends, and at his age, his friends and social engagements keep growing," Darcy noted. "I should not be surprised if he were to give up Netherfield as soon as any reasonable offer on the estate is made."

Elizabeth made no answer. She was afraid of talking too much about his friend and his treatment of her sister. Instead, she decided it was up to him to lead the conversation. He took the hint, and said, as he gazed around

. . . Something, Anything, to Say

the drawing room, "This seems a very comfortable house. Lady Catherine, I believe, did a great deal to it when Mr. Collins first came to Hunsford. Mr. Collins also appears very fortunate in his choice of a wife," he added politely.

"Yes, indeed. His friends may rejoice in his having met one of the very few sensible women who would have accepted him. Charlotte is very smart, though I am not certain that I consider her marrying Mr. Collins the wisest thing she ever did. She seems perfectly happy, however. In purely economic terms, it is certainly a good match for her," stated Elizabeth frankly.

"It must be very nice for her to be settled not too far from her own family and friends," Darcy said.

"An easy distance?" Elizabeth asked incredulously. "It is nearly fifty miles! It's not that a woman must always be close to her family. If one has money, distance becomes unimportant.

But that's not the case here. Mr. And Mrs. Collins have a comfortable income, but not one that allows for frequent travel."

Mr. Darcy drew his chair a little towards her. "Do you have such a strong attachment to Longbourn?" he asked.

Elizabeth was surprised at his question. She started to reply, but her words were cut short by the arrival of Charlotte and her sister, who were returning from their walk. Finding Darcy there surprised them. Mr. Darcy explained his own surprise at his having found Miss Bennet alone. Then, after wishing the ladies a good day, he left.

"What can be the meaning of this!" asked Charlotte, as soon as he was gone. "Eliza, he must be in love with you, or he would never have called on us in this familiar way!"

But Elizabeth heartily disagreed. She felt he had nothing but contempt for her and her family. Thus, Mr. Darcy's visits to the parsonage remained a mystery. It wasn't her company,

Elizabeth Laughed at the Idea.

Elizabeth decided, as he frequently sat for ten minutes without saying a single word!

Charlotte had once or twice suggested to Elizabeth that Darcy was interested in her, but Elizabeth always laughed at the idea. As a result, Charlotte didn't press the subject. She didn't want to raise her friend's expectations, lest they end in disappointment.

In fact, in her kind schemes for Elizabeth, she planned for her to marry Colonel Fitzwilliam. He had much to offer: a pleasing manner and an excellent position in society. But unlike Mr. Darcy, he had no influence in the church, which was of great interest to the new Mrs. Collins. Perhaps Mr. Darcy was the man for Elizabeth after all!

CHAPTER 13

An Unusual Courtship

It seemed strange to Elizabeth that she should always meet Mr. Darcy in her rambles through the park. At first, she thought it a coincidence. Then, to prevent it from happening again, she told him it was a favorite haunt of hers, hoping to scare him off. When she met him a second time, she thought it very odd.

By the third encounter, she was puzzled. Why had he asked her so many questions—how she felt about Hunsford, her love of walks,

She Was Puzzled.

her opinion of the Collins' happiness? He even implied she would stay at Rosings whenever she returned to the area. Did he assume she would marry Colonel Fitzwilliam?

One day, as she walked, instead of being surprised by Mr. Darcy, she saw Colonel Fitzwilliam. Since they were friends, they could candidly discuss anything—their friends, money, marriage, and the effect wealth had on marriage prospects and happiness.

"Sadly, younger sons cannot marry who they like," he shrugged, "since oldest sons inherit all the property."

"Unless they like women of fortune," said Elizabeth, "which they often do."

"There are not many in my position who can afford to marry without some attention to money," he admitted.

"Is this," thought Elizabeth, "meant for me?" and she blushed. "I wonder that Mr. Darcy does not marry," she said bluntly. "But perhaps his sister's company is enough for now. And

Mr. Darcy, of course, is a great friend of Mr. Bingley."

"I agree! From something Darcy told me recently, though he didn't mention any names, I have reason to think Bingley is indebted to him," the colonel said.

"What is it you mean?" Elizabeth asked eagerly, thinking of Jane. Would she finally learn the truth behind Bingley's abrupt departure?

"He said he saved a friend from a bad marriage. I thought it might be Bingley, because he's the kind of chap who would get into a scrape of that sort."

"Did Mr. Darcy give you his reasons for interfering?" Elizabeth asked.

"There were strong objections against the lady," Fitzwilliam murmured. After watching her a little, Fitzwilliam asked her why she was so serious.

"I'm appalled by your cousin's conduct. Why should he judge others? What right does Mr.

Strong Objections Against the Lady

Darcy have to decide if his friend is happy?"

Anxious not to arouse his suspicions, she changed the subject, talking of indifferent matters until they reached the parsonage. Once alone, she could think about all she had learned. He must be speaking of Bingley. There could not exist in the world two men over whom Mr. Darcy could have such influence!

His interferences were the cause of Jane's suffering. He had ruined her hope for happiness.

"There were strong objections against the lady," were Colonel Fitzwilliam's words, and these strong objections were probably family-oriented.

"No one could object to Jane herself," Elizabeth exclaimed to herself. "She is lovely and good and well-mannered." Of course, Elizabeth was acutely aware of the embarrassment her mother often caused publicly, but she didn't suppose that carried any weight with Mr. Darcy. His pride would only be wounded by

Jane's lack of social connections.

Elizabeth concluded that Darcy's pride, coupled with his wish to have Mr. Bingley for his sister, had caused the separation between Bingley and Jane. That realization made her sick, and she refused to accompany her cousins to Rosings. From now on, she would refuse to see Mr. Darcy!

Darcy's Pride Caused the Separation.

CHAPTER 14

Love is Revealed

Elizabeth's one consolation was that she would soon be leaving Hunsford. Mr. Darcy's shameful boast of the misery he had caused heightened her sense of Jane's suffering. At least she would not have to see him again. Instead, she would soon be home with Jane.

She was suddenly roused by the sound of the door bell, and her spirits were raised, thinking it might be Colonel Fitzwilliam. Then, to her utter amazement, she saw Mr. Darcy walk into the room. He asked how she was, and she answered him coldly.

Darcy then began pacing the room. Elizabeth was surprised, but said nothing. After a silence of several minutes, he approached her. He looked upset and his words came fast and furious.

"I can't keep my feelings to myself any longer. I have to tell you the truth. I am deeply in love with you!" he cried.

Elizabeth's astonishment left her speechless. She stared at him, blushed, but said nothing. He talked about how much he cared for her, even as he described her inferior social standing. His words may have been honest, but the insult to her family did not endear Darcy to Elizabeth.

In spite of her deeply rooted dislike of him, she was aware of the compliments he paid her. And, though she could not dream of being his wife, she did not want to cause him pain. He concluded by stressing the strength of his

"Will You Marry Me?" He Asked at Last.

attachment to her. In spite of all the obstacles between them, he explained, she had conquered his heart.

"Will you marry me?" he asked at last.

"I know I am supposed to thank you for your love, even if it is not welcome. If I could feel gratitude, I would thank you. But I cannot. I have never cared what you thought of me. I'll tell you exactly why now!" Elizabeth exclaimed.

Mr. Darcy, who was leaning against the mantelpiece, was surprised at what she said. He could not believe what he was hearing! She had turned him down? Impossible! He struggled to compose himself, then spoke in a voice of forced calmness.

"May I ask why you have rejected me? And why it was done so coldly?"

"I might ask the same," she replied. "Why did you insult me? Why did you say you liked me against your will? But you know I have still other reasons," she cried. "Do you really think

I would ever marry the man who has ruined, perhaps forever, the happiness of my sister?"

As she spoke, Mr. Darcy changed color. He listened intently, however, and did not try to interrupt her.

"I have every reason in the world to think badly of you. You cannot deny that you have been the main reason, if not the *only* reason, for dividing Jane and Mr. Bingley. Do you have any idea how much misery you've caused?"

She paused, and saw that he was listening to her. Still, he did not show an ounce of remorse.

"Can you deny that you have done it?" she repeated.

"I do not deny that I did everything in my power to separate my friend from your sister. I also rejoice in my success," he boasted.

Elizabeth was so angry that her rage poured out. "Jane is not the only reason I refuse to marry you. My opinion of you was decided long before that. Your actions resulted in misfortune for Mr. Wickham. In what imaginary act

"Every Reason in the World."

PRIDE AND PREJUDICE

of friendship can you defend yourself on that score?"

"His misfortunes," sneered Darcy, "have been great indeed."

"Thanks to you!" cried Elizabeth with energy. "You reduced him to poverty. You have withheld the gifts promised him. Yet you make fun of his misfortunes!"

"This", cried Darcy, as he walked with quick steps across the room, "is your opinion of me! This is the low opinion in which you hold me! I thank you for explaining it so fully. I must ask you: Could you really expect me to be happy about your lack of social connections?"

Elizabeth felt herself growing more angry every moment. "I don't want to hear any more from you. Nothing in the world would tempt me to accept you." Again his astonishment was obvious. He could scarcely believe her words, yet he was terribly upset by her strong rejection.

"From the first moment I saw you," she went

on, "I hated your arrogance, your conceit and your insensitivity to others. I felt that you were the last man in the world I would ever marry!"

"You have said enough," Darcy thundered. "I understand your feelings, and am only ashamed of what my own have been." And with these words he hastily left the room. Elizabeth heard him open the front door and flee the house.

Her mind was rushing. What a scene! She was amazed at what had happened. Mr. Darcy had proposed to her! He had been in love with her for months! So much in love that he was willing to marry her in spite of his objections. Those same objections he had to Bingley's marrying Jane. The force of his love was incredible!

Then Elizabeth remembered his pride, what he had done with respect to Jane, and his cruelty to Mr. Wickham—none of which he denied. Whatever pity she had for Darcy vanished.

A Walk in Her Favorite Park

CHAPTER 15

A Letter of Explanation

Elizabeth awoke the next morning to the same thoughts and puzzlement. It was impossible to think of anything else. She decided to take a walk in her favorite park, hoping to be alone with her thoughts.

After walking two or three times along the lane, she was tempted to stop at the gates. There she caught a glimpse of a gentleman in the grove. But the person was near enough to see her, and stepping forward eagerly, was calling her name. It was Mr. Darcy!

He held out a letter, which she immediately took. With a look of great seriousness he said, "I have been walking in the hope of meeting you. Will you do me the honor of reading this letter?" And then, with a slight bow, he turned toward the house and disappeared.

With the strongest curiosity, Elizabeth opened the letter. It held two sheets of paper. It was dated from Rosings, at eight o'clock in the morning, and was as follows:

"Dear Miss Bennet:
"You have charged me with two offenses. The first: My ending the relationship between Mr. Bingley and your sister. The second: My part in Mr. Wickham's misfortunes. I am sorry if anything I say here will cause you pain, but I want you to know the truth. I acted as I did for a good reason.

Here is what happened with your sister: I hadn't been in Hampshire long before I saw

He Held Out a Letter.

how much Bingley liked your eldest sister. I had often seen him in love before. I watched my friend closely, and could see how much he openly cared for her. I also watched Jane. She was open and cheerful and engaging—but she didn't seem particularly interested in Bingley. I was convinced therefore, that though Jane was a lovely girl, Bingley's passion for her was not returned. Since you claim otherwise, I must be in error. If so, I can fully understand why you resent me.

I can only say in my defense, that Jane's behavior suggested to me that she was not in love with my friend. Thus, I feared he would enter into a marriage without love and desire. But, in truth, I had other objections. Your mother's family has no social standing, but that was nothing in comparison to the lack of properness shown by her and your three younger sisters.

The part which I acted is now to be explained. I will add that Bingley's sisters agreed with me. I do not think your family's behavior would have prevented the marriage had he not been convinced of your sister's indifference to him. Bingley had thought she did care for him, but he greatly relies on my judgment.

I convinced him that his passion was not returned. I do not blame myself for having done this. I thought I was doing the right thing. The only thing I do blame myself for is concealing from him that Jane was in London. He knew nothing of her visit there. Please know that I acted only out of concern for my friend; I had no wish to hurt your sister.

With respect to Mr. Wickham, I can only tell you his connection with my family. Mr. Wickham is the son of a very respectable man, who managed the Pemberley estates for many years. Wickham was my father's godson and he supported him at school and at Cambridge. He hoped the church would be his profession and intended to provide him a living in it.

"I Was Prepared to Help Him."

My father died about five years ago. His attachment to Mr. Wickham was strong, and he wrote in his will that he would like me to promote his advancement. If he took holy orders, I was to give him a valuable family parish. There was also a legacy of one thousand pounds.

Mr. Wickham wrote eventually to tell me that he decided against taking orders. He did, however, intend to study the law. I must know, he stated, that the interest of one thousand pounds could not support that decision. I was prepared to help him. We settled it between ourselves. I knew him as my father did not to be a man without principle. I knew he ought not to be a clergyman. Thus, when Wickham gave up the church, in return, I gave him three thousand pounds. All connection between us was now dissolved.

His plan to study law was a pretense—he led a life full of idleness and drunkenness. I heard nothing of him for three years. Then, when the clergyman of the parish which had been earmarked for him died, Wickham wrote to me. His circumstances, he assured me, were very bad. He had found the law an unprofitable study and now wanted to be a minister, if I would give him the parish in question, as I was aware of my dear father's intentions.

You will hardly blame me for refusing to agree with this demand. He resented me and took out his rage at me on my sister. What I am about to tell you I trust you will hold in utter secrecy. Last summer, he sought out my sister, who is ten years my junior. She was with her teacher in Ramsgate. He courted my sister, a child of fifteen. She thought herself in love and he persuaded her to elope with him! Happily, my sister and I are close and she told me what she planned to do a day before the elopement. I wrote to Wickham, who immediately left town. I knew that his chief object was my sister's fortune, which is thirty thousand pounds. But I also suspect that he wanted to revenge

"You Will Hardly Blame Me."

himself on me. If you need to verify the truth of this letter, please ask Colonel Fitzwilliam. He is one of the executors of my father's will.

Yours truly,
Fitzwilliam Darcy"

CHAPTER 16

Thinking About the Past

Elizabeth was completely overwhelmed by Darcy's letter. She didn't think he was sorry for all the pain he had caused Jane. She could not believe Darcy's thinking that Jane had acted indifferently to Bingley. Anyone who had ever seen them together knew how they both felt. His interference in Bingley's affairs was all about his pride, his sense of dignity and his notions of his friend's proper place in society. It was nothing more.

Wickham, however, was a more complicated

"One of Those Men Is Lying to Me."

case. Darcy's explanation of Wickham's connection to his family was exactly what Wickham had told her himself. Moreover, what Wickham had said of the parish was still fresh in her mind.

"I feel that one of those men is lying to me," she thought. "But every time I read and re-read the part in the letter about Wickham resigning and receiving money, I hesitate."

She thought carefully of all Wickham had told her, and all Darcy had written. She was forced to conclude that Mr. Darcy, who she once thought mean, was innocent of all charges. She realized how odd it was that Wickham should have told his story to her, a total stranger.

In truth, she had never heard of Wickham before his entrance into the militia. Nothing had been known to them about his former life except what he said himself. She tried to remember one instance of goodness or integrity in Wickham that might rescue him from Mr. Darcy's attack, but she could not think of any.

Elizabeth tried to remember the conversations she and Wickham had had. She remembered that he boasted of having no fear of seeing Mr. Darcy—yet it was Wickham who had avoided the Netherfield ball the very next week. She also remembered that until the Bingleys and Darcy had left Netherfield, he had not uttered a word of his story! It was only after their departure, when they could not disprove his claims, that Wickham had launched his attack on Darcy!

What a different light this put him in. Clearly he had stopped courting Elizabeth when he learned of her financial state. Every former good feeling evaporated. She had been ill-used by him. She now knew that Darcy was telling the truth about Wickham.

Suddenly, Elizabeth felt ashamed of herself. Darcy was prideful, but she had been prejudiced! "How horribly I have acted," she cried. "Vanity, not love, has been my folly. I who pride

Every Good Feeling Evaporated.

myself on intelligence. I have courted prejudice and ignorance. I drove away reason wherever I saw it!"

Her thoughts flew from herself to Jane and from Jane to Bingley. Was Darcy right about Jane, too? He said he was unaware of Jane's feelings. She was forced to admit the truth of that statement—even Charlotte had told Jane she should not conceal her true feelings from Bingley!

As for his other charge, her family's lack of manners, she had only to remember her mother's behavior at the Netherfield ball. Despite her embarrassment, she could not deny that Darcy was right. Oh, how wrong she had been about everything!

She thought again of Bingley. Now that she knew his true feelings for Jane, it heightened the sense of what Jane had lost. His affection had proven sincere. He had wanted to marry her sister, but had not been sure of her feelings for him. How horrid that Jane had been deprived of happiness by her own restraint and her family's lack of social grace!

To these thoughts were added the realization of Wickham's true character. He had deceived her. Painfully unhappy, she spent each day until her departure studying Mr. Darcy's letter. Soon, she knew it almost by heart. Though she appreciated his attachment to her, she was still at odds with him. But would she ever even see him again?

Mr. Darcy and Colonel Fitzwilliam left Rosings the next morning. Elizabeth made her arrangements to return to Longbourn. Her one consolation was going home. She parted from Lady Catherine, who wished her a good journey and invited her to come to Hunsford again next year.

It was the second week in May when Elizabeth returned home. Her sisters were delighted to see her. Kitty and Lydia quickly filled her in on all the local gossip.

"I have some interesting news," said Lydia

Her Younger Sisters Talked Endlessly.

triumphantly. "There is no danger of Wickham's marrying Mary King. She is gone down to her uncle at Liverpool. Dear Wickham is safe."

"And Mary King is safe!" added Elizabeth, "safe from a man who only loves her money!"

While her younger sisters talked endlessly about the love affairs of the army officers, Elizabeth told Jane all the exciting news about Mr. Darcy. "I thought I was so clever, disliking him so," Elizabeth admitted. "Dislike sometimes sharpens one's wit."

"He must be extremely disappointed that you refused him," Jane said.

"Indeed," replied Elizabeth, "I am sorry if I caused him pain. You don't blame me for refusing him, do you?"

"Blame you! Oh, no."

"There is something else," she added, and told her sister all she had learned about George Wickham from Mr. Darcy. "I want to ask you, Jane. Do you think I ought to make

PRIDE AND PREJUDICE

people aware of Wickham's true character? For my part, I am inclined to believe Mr. Darcy," concluded Elizabeth, "but what shall I do? There was clearly great mismanagement in the education of those two young men. One has got all the goodness, and the other has all the appearance of it!" she said, shaking her head in wonder.

Jane paused a little and then replied, "Surely, there can be no need for our exposing him so dreadfully. What do you think?"

"That it ought not to be attempted. Mr. Darcy swore me to secrecy. Wickham will soon be gone; therefore, no one need know what he is *really* like."

"You are quite right," Jane nodded. "To have his errors made public might ruin him forever."

What Elizabeth didn't reveal to Jane was the rest of Darcy's letter. She didn't tell her how much Bingley loved her. It pained her to keep this secret, since she knew Jane was unhappy. Her sister, after an eight-month separation,

It Pained Her to Keep This Secret.

still cherished a tender love for Bingley.

If Bingley was on Jane's mind, the departure of the regiment from Meryton occupied the thoughts of the other young ladies in the neighborhood. Kitty and Lydia Bennet were nearly hysterical. They fretted that their endless social whirl had come to an end.

"Good heavens! What is to become of us! What are we to do!" Lydia exclaimed bitterly.

"If we could just go to Brighton!" observed Mrs. Bennet. She and Lydia had been invited to that lively seaside resort by Colonel and Mrs. Forster.

"Oh, yes!" agreed Lydia, "if we could go to Brighton! But papa refuses to take a holiday at the seaside!"

Such were the complaints that resounded throughout the Bennet house. Elizabeth could almost hear Darcy's objections to her family's silly remarks. So annoying were they that she could almost forgive him his interference in Bingley's life. To be saddled with such a shallow family! Elizabeth decided to speak to her father about the situation.

"If you were aware," said Elizabeth, "of the very great disadvantage Lydia's manners give us!"

"Has she frightened away some of your suitors?" smiled Mr. Bennet.

"Father, our respectability in the world is affected by her wild character. If you do not restrain her, she'll be beyond reach. Her character will be fixed, and she will, at sixteen, be the most outrageous flirt. She makes herself and the family look ridiculous! She is vain, idle and uncontrollable!"

"Do not make yourself uneasy, my dear. Rest assured, you and Jane are respected and valued wherever you go. But we shall have no peace at Longbourn if Lydia does *not* go to Brighton. Colonel Forster is a sensible man, and he will keep her out of any real mischief. Don't forget," he said wagging his finger at her, "she is too poor for a young man to pursue. Let

Surprised, Displeased and Alarmed

us hope the Brighton visit will teach her how unimportant she really is!"

Elizabeth was forced to be content with his answer. Her mother and Lydia soon left for Brighton. Elizabeth, meanwhile, decided to see Mr. Wickham for the last time.

On the very last day of the regiment's stay in Meryton, a party was held in the barracks. Wickham sat with Elizabeth. He asked how she had enjoyed Hunsford, and she mentioned Colonel Fitzwilliam and Mr. Darcy being at Rosings. "Do you know Colonel Fitzwilliam?" she asked.

He looked surprised, displeased and alarmed. He replied that he believed Fitzwilliam to be a gentleman. Did Elizabeth like him?

"His manners are very different from Mr. Darcy's," she said, "but I like Mr. Darcy the more I get to know him."

"Really!" cried Wickham with a wild look in his eye.

"What I mean is that the more I get to know him, the more I understand why he acts as he does," Elizabeth explained.

Wickham was looking more and more nervous and alarmed by the minute. "I assume that he merely gives the *appearance* of doing what is right. That is different from doing the right thing. I just hope his pride will prevent him in future from harming others as he has harmed me."

Elizabeth could not repress a smile at hearing this. They said their goodbyes politely, though both secretly hoped they had seen the last of the other! When the dinner ended, Lydia returned with Mrs. Forster to Meryton. She was to travel on to Brighton the next day.

Polite Goodbyes

CHAPTER 17

Visit to Pemberley

Elizabeth, who was not interested in going to Brighton, used the time to study her own family. She was forced to admit that her parents did not have a very happy marriage.

Her father had been captivated by youth and beauty, and had married a woman with a weak mind and selfish heart. Thus, early in their marriage, he had lost all real affection for her. Respect, esteem and confidence had vanished and all his hopes for marital happiness were lost. He took solace in nature and his books. His wife and her foolish ideas did not interest him.

Even as she despaired of her parents, Elizabeth rejoiced over Wickham's departure. But at home, there was constant complaining. To keep her spirits up, she eagerly accepted an invitation from the Gardiners to travel with them.

The next week, the Gardiners arrived in Longbourn to pick up Elizabeth and head north for Derbyshire. Elizabeth was excited and curious. Would it be possible to see the great houses of Derbyshire without seeing Mr. Darcy and his Pemberley?

Off the trio went, through Oxford, Warwick, and Birmingham. When they finally arrived at the little town of Lambton, they stopped to explore all the wonders of the countryside. Her aunt, a native of Derbyshire, expressed a desire to see Pemberley again.

"My dear, would you like to see a place you have heard so much about?" asked her aunt.

They Drove Through a Beautiful Wood.

"Wickham spent his youth there, you know."

Elizabeth was very distressed. She felt she had no business at Pemberley, now that she had refused Mr. Darcy's offer of marriage. But her aunt insisted. "The grounds are delightful and it has some of the finest woods in the country."

Elizabeth said no more. The possibility of meeting Mr. Darcy haunted her. It would be dreadful. She blushed at the very idea. But she was afraid to speak openly to her aunt. Thus, to Pemberley they would go!

Elizabeth, as they drove along, watched for the first appearance of Pemberley Woods with some nervousness. By the time they had reached the lodge, she had butterflies in her stomach. They entered the grounds in one of its lowest points, and drove for some time through a beautiful wood, stretching over a wide extent.

Elizabeth's mind was much too full for conversation, but she saw and admired every remarkable spot and point of view. Then her eye was caught by Pemberley House, situated on the opposite side of a valley, framed by a winding road. It was a large, handsome, stone building and backed by a ridge of high woody hills. In front of the house was a stream.

Elizabeth was delighted. She had never seen an estate where nature had been so neatly enhanced by architecture. She and her relatives were all warm in their admiration. At that moment, she felt that to be mistress of Pemberley would be something!

They descended the hill, crossed the bridge and drove to the door. Her fears of meeting its owner returned. On asking for a tour of the house, they waited for the housekeeper to show them around.

The housekeeper came, a respectable-looking, elderly woman. The rooms were lofty and handsome, and their furniture suitable to Darcy's considerable fortune. Elizabeth had to admire his taste; there was less splendor and

Her Eye Was Caught by Pemberley House.

more real elegance than at Rosings.

"And of this place," thought she, "I might have been mistress! With these rooms, I might now have been familiarly acquainted! Instead of viewing them as a stranger, I might have enjoyed them as my own, and welcomed my aunt and uncle as my visitors to this great house."

Mr. Gardiner, whose manners were easy and pleasant, encouraged the housekeeper to talk. Mrs. Reynolds, either from pride or attachment, took great pleasure in talking of her master and his sister.

"Is your master much at Pemberley in the course of the year?" Mr. Gardiner asked.

"Not so much as I could wish, sir."

"If your master would marry, you might see more of him," Mr. Gardiner hinted.

"Yes, sir; but I do not know when that will be. I do not know who is good enough for him." Mr. and Mrs. Gardiner smiled at the housekeeper's pride in Mr. Darcy.

"I have never had a cross word from him in my life, and I have known him ever since he was four years old."

This was praise that conflicted with Elizabeth's own ideas. She had long believed that he was not a good-tempered man. She longed to hear more.

"He is the best landlord, and the best master," said Mrs. Reynolds proudly. "Not like the wild young men nowadays, who think of nothing but themselves. There is not one of his tenants or servants who would not speak well of him. Some people call him proud, but I am sure I never saw anything of that. To my fancy, it is only because he does not rattle away like other young men."

"This puts him in a much better light!" thought Elizabeth.

"This fine account of him," whispered her aunt, as they walked, "is not quite consistent with his behavior to Wickham."

"Perhaps we have been deceived," Elizabeth

A Tour of the Grounds

whispered back. If only they knew!

After all, Elizabeth thought, the praise bestowed on him by Mrs. Reynolds was of no small nature. What praise is more valuable than the praise of an intelligent servant? As a brother, a landlord, and master, she considered how many people's happiness was in his hands! How much pleasure or pain it was in his power to bestow!

When all of the house that was open to the general public was seen, they were taken on a tour of the grounds by a gardener, who met them at the hall door. As they walked across the lawn towards the river, Elizabeth turned back to look at Pemberley once more. Suddenly, Darcy appeared in the road behind the stables!

She had instinctively turned away, but turned back, as he spoke to her. Elizabeth blushed deeply. Neither of them were at ease. Her aunt and uncle, who had been walking with the gardener, returned. They both commented on the handsome figure Darcy made as he walked away.

Elizabeth, for her part, was overpowered by emotion. Her coming there, she suspected, was the worst idea in the world! That he should even speak to her was amazing—and to speak as he did. She realized that he had never spoken to her before with such gentleness.

If only she knew what he was thinking! Did he still love her? Elizabeth kept her thoughts to herself. When her relations wanted to continue their walk, she nodded her agreement.

While wandering in this slow, lazy manner, they were again surprised. Mr. Darcy was again approaching them. Elizabeth admired his good manners. To match such politeness, she complimented him on the beauty of Pemberley.

Mrs. Gardiner was standing a little behind her niece. Darcy asked if Elizabeth would do him the honor of introducing him. She could hardly suppress a smile at his wanting to meet

Darcy Was Again Approaching Them!

some of the very people his pride had revolted against earlier!

The introduction, however, was immediately made. When she told him that the Gardiners were her aunt and uncle, it was clear he was pleased by the connection. He responded with great courtesy and began speaking to Mr. Gardiner. Elizabeth could not help but be happy, even triumphant. It was important to her for him to know that she had relatives she was proud of.

The conversation soon turned to fishing. "Please feel free to fish on my property as much as you like while you visit Derbyshire," Darcy said. "I will be happy to provide you with all the necessary equipment."

Elizabeth said nothing, but understood that the invitation was clearly a compliment to her. Why, she wondered, can he still be in love with me?

Mrs. Gardiner, tired from the walk, soon turned to her husband for support. Mr. Darcy walked beside Elizabeth and after a short silence, Elizabeth spoke. She wanted him to know that she assumed he would not be at home and that she was surprised by his appearance.

He explained that business had been the reason for his early arrival and that in a few hours his friends, Mr. Bingley and his sisters, would join him. "There is also one other person in the party," he continued after a pause, "who wants to meet you. May I introduce you to my sister during your stay here?"

"I'd be most pleased to meet her," she said, happy that he did not think badly of her, as she had feared.

Mr. and Mrs. Gardiner were invited into the house for refreshments, but they declined with the utmost politeness. Mr. Darcy handed the ladies into the carriage, and when it drove off, Elizabeth saw him walking slowly towards the house.

"He is perfectly well-behaved, polite and

"Some May Call Him Proud."

unassuming," said her uncle.

"There is something a little stately in him," replied her aunt, "but though some people may call him proud, I have seen nothing of it."

"Why did you tell us he was so disagreeable, Lizzy?" her uncle asked.

Elizabeth excused herself, explaining that she had never seen him as pleasant as he was that morning. She felt she should say something to explain his true treatment of Wickham. So she told them that reliable sources had informed her that his actions toward Wickham were of the most honorable kind.

Mrs. Gardiner was surprised and concerned, but said nothing. Elizabeth was too amazed by the day's events to say more. All she could think of was Darcy and his wish that she meet his sister. What could this mean?

CHAPTER 18

A Change of Heart

Elizabeth had agreed that Mr. Darcy would bring his sister to visit the very day after she reached Pemberley. But it was not to be. On the very morning after her own arrival in Lambton, Darcy's carriage came to take Elizabeth to Pemberley. Her aunt and uncle were astounded. They could only assume by Mr. Darcy's constant attention to Elizabeth that he was very much in love with her.

To the Gardiners, it was evident that while

Darcy's Carriage Appeared.

Elizabeth's feelings were unknown, Mr. Darcy was clearly smitten with her. Some, they thought, might accuse him of pride, but it was known that he was a liberal man and was kind to the poor. They also learned that Wickham had left debts behind him in Derbyshire—and that Darcy had paid them.

Georgiana Darcy stepped out and the introduction took place. Elizabeth had heard that Miss Darcy was proud, but, in fact, she actually was quite shy! Though little more than sixteen, she was taller than Elizabeth and graceful and sweet.

They had not been together long when Bingley and his sister arrived. He was very happy to see Elizabeth and immediately asked after her family. Elizabeth wondered if he was still in love with Jane. One thing was clear: Miss Darcy was not a rival to Jane. There was nothing in the way the two looked at each other or spoke to each other that could justify the hopes of Bingley's sisters. Miss Darcy was clearly not going to be his wife!

Bingley tapped Elizabeth on the shoulder to get her attention. "You know," he said in a tone of real regret, "it has been a very long time since I had the pleasure of seeing Jane. I even remember the date of our last meeting."

While Elizabeth was gratified that he still asked after Jane, she was almost stunned by Mr. Darcy's attentions to her.

His manners were so wonderful. He wasn't proud or disdainful. He was gentle and attentive. Never in all the times she had seen him had he been so eager to please!

She now realized that she still meant something to him. Could she still ever get him to propose to her again?

Even as Elizabeth pondered this question, she was forced to deal with another. Since coming to Pemberley, she was convinced that Miss Bingley's dislike of her was due to jealousy. The latter never missed a chance to insult Elizabeth or the Bennet family.

Miss Bingley Began Expressing Her Dislike.

"Pray, Miss Eliza, haven't the militia left Meryton? They must be a *great* loss to your family," jabbed Miss Bingley.

She would not dare mention Wickham's name in Darcy's presence, but her tone was unmistakable. As she spoke, Elizabeth noticed that Darcy and his sister seemed embarrassed.

Had Miss Bingley known what pain she was giving her friends? Or was she just interested in unsettling Elizabeth, since she thought her to be Wickham's special friend?

Elizabeth, out of regard for Miss Darcy's ill-fated romantic venture, refused to speak. Instead, she left shortly thereafter. Mr. Darcy went to help her into the carriage. As soon as she left, Miss Bingley began expressing her dislike of Elizabeth. Georgiana Darcy would not join in, so when Mr. Darcy returned, Miss Bingley again repeated her nasty comments.

"I must confess that I never could see any beauty in her," she said. "Her face is too thin, her complexion is not bright. She has a shrewish look." Of course, Miss Bingley had her heart set on winning Darcy for herself. Alas, she did not realize that insulting her rival was an unwise course!

So she was devastated when he replied, "I consider her one of the handsomest women I know."

He then went away, and Miss Bingley was left with the pain she had brought on herself.

That night, Elizabeth could think only about Darcy. She was ashamed of ever disliking him. She knew she respected and cared about him. She was grateful that he not only had loved her, but that by his actions, had clearly forgiven her for the mean way in which she had rejected his marriage proposal. His wish for her to meet his sister was a great compliment. Perhaps all was not lost!

"One of the Handsomest Women"

CHAPTER 19

Scandal!

As much as Elizabeth was enjoying her visit to Lambton, she longed to hear from Jane. When a letter finally arrived, it was filled with distressing news. Jane wrote to say that Lydia, their high-spirited sister, had run off with Wickham! Mrs. Bennet was beside herself and their father was frantic.

"Everyone believes the worst. We only hope that they will be married quickly, since they seemed to have disappeared without a trace!"

wrote Jane.

"Oh! Where, where is my uncle?" cried Elizabeth, darting from her seat as she finished the letter. But as she reached the door, it was opened by a servant, and Mr. Darcy appeared. Her pale face and upset manner alarmed him.

"Good God! What is the matter?" he cried. "I'll have the servant send for the Gardiners."

Elizabeth hesitated, but her knees trembled under her. She sat down, unable to support herself, and looking so ill that it was impossible for Darcy to leave her.

"I am all right. I am only distressed by some dreadful news which I have just received from Longbourn."

She suddenly burst into tears and for a few minutes could not speak another word. Darcy sat beside her in compassionate silence. At length, she spoke again.

"I have terrible news. My youngest sister has left and eloped with Mr. Wickham! They have gone off together from Brighton. You know him

"She Is Lost Forever!"

too well to doubt the rest. She has no money, no connections, nothing that can keep him with her. She is lost for ever!"

"I am very sorry," cried Darcy. "Are you absolutely certain?"

"Oh yes! They left Brighton together on Sunday night, and no one has heard a word," Elizabeth sobbed.

"And what has been done to find her?" he asked.

"My father has gone to London to seek my uncle's help. But nothing can be done. How can they cope with such a man?"

Darcy shook his head in silent agreement. Looking at him, she realized how much his strength and kindness meant to her. Never had she felt before how much she could have loved him! But she could not think about herself. She must think about Lydia—the humiliation and the misery she was bringing upon herself and her family.

Darcy waited for her to collect herself, then

spoke with gentle restraint. "I wish to heaven there was something I might do."

"Just please keep this news to yourself," begged Elizabeth. "Conceal the unhappy truth as long as possible. I will leave for home today."

As she finished speaking, her uncle arrived. Darcy bowed and excused himself. Elizabeth wondered about Lydia. When did she become friendly with Wickham? Why had she done such a reckless thing? At the same time, Elizabeth thought of Darcy. Would she ever see him again?

"I have been thinking it over again, Elizabeth," said her uncle as they drove from the town. "It is unlikely that Wickham would ruin a girl staying with the colonel's family. Could he expect that her friends would not step forward? Could he expect to be kept in the regiment after such an affront to Colonel Forster?"

"Do you really think there is hope?" cried Elizabeth, brightening up for a moment.

"Do You Really Think There Is Hope?"

"Upon my word," said Mrs. Gardiner, "I agree with your uncle. It is really too great a violation of decency and honor to think of his doing anything else."

"But why all this secrecy? Why the fear of detection? Why must their marriage be private?" asked Elizabeth. "Wickham will never marry a woman without some money! He cannot afford it."

"You think Lydia is so lost to everything but love of him that she would stay with him without being married?" asked her shocked aunt.

"Frankly, I don't know what to think," replied Elizabeth. "Perhaps I am not doing her justice. But she is very young and has been allowed to behave in the most idle and frivolous manner."

They traveled as quickly as possible and sleeping one night on the road, reached Longbourn by dinner the next day. It was a comfort to Elizabeth to be home.

Elizabeth jumped from the carriage and ran

straight to Jane. "Is there any news?" The sisters embraced tearfully.

"Not yet," replied Jane. "Mother hasn't left her bedroom. Come and see her at once."

Mrs. Bennet received them with tears and cries of regret. She blamed everyone but herself for Lydia's conduct. "If I had been able," she said, "to go to Brighton this would not have happened! Why did the Forsters ever let her out of their sight?"

Mr. Gardiner tried to reassure his sister, explaining to her that he meant to be in London the very next day, and would assist Mr. Bennet in finding Lydia.

"Oh! My dear brother," replied Mrs. Bennet, "When you get to town, find them, wherever they may be. If they are not married already, make them marry! Above all, keep Mr. Bennet from fighting. Tell him I am frightened out of my wits."

Jane and Elizabeth went to their own room. Elizabeth longed to tell her sister all that had

All Their Concerns Had to be About Lydia.

happened. But this was not the time. Now all their concerns had to be about Lydia, her safety and her situation. Because of her thoughtless, foolish behavior, they might possibly never hold their heads up again.

If Darcy had thought little of her family before, Elizabeth could not bear the thought of what he must be thinking now. All thoughts of Darcy, and of Pemberley, and bright hopes for the future, must be forgotten. Most of all, Lydia had to be found.

Even poor Jane's loss of Bingley was nothing compared to this.

CHAPTER 20

Lydia is Married

The whole family hoped for a letter from Mr. Bennet the next morning, but nothing came. Mr. Gardiner had waited only for the mail before setting off. Mrs. Bennet fretted needlessly that her husband might be killed in a duel.

Meanwhile, all Meryton condemned Wickham, the man they once adored. It was said he had left debts to every tradesman in town. Everyone said he was the wickedest young

Mrs. Bennet Fretted Needlessly.

man in the world!

Each day that passed at Longbourn was filled with anxiety. The Bennets lived only for news of Lydia. Finally, Mr. Gardiner wrote to say that their father was coming home. He had not been able to locate Lydia. Mrs. Bennet was beside herself. "Who will fight Wickham and make him marry Lydia if he comes home?" she wailed.

Fortunately, they didn't have to wait long for an answer. Two days after Mr. Bennet's return, a letter came from Mr. Gardiner. Mr. Bennet was so worried he had Elizabeth read the letter aloud. It said:

"My Dear Brother:

"I have seen them both. They are not married. But I hope they will marry before too long. All that is required of you is to assure Lydia that you will still give her her equal share of the five thousand pounds left on your death. Also, that you give her one hundred pounds a year. I think this is reasonable.

"Mr. Wickham's circumstances aren't as hopeless as we thought. If you give me the power to act in your name, the whole business will be settled as quickly as possible. We have decided that it is best that Lydia should be married in my house.

"Yours, Edward Gardiner"

The good news quickly spread throughout the neighborhood.

For her part, Elizabeth was now sorry that she had made Mr. Darcy acquainted with her fears for her sister, since the marriage would hopefully conceal the scandal of the elopement. She had no fear of his revealing any details. There were few people on whose secrecy she could so confidently depend. Still, she was humiliated that he knew so much about her family.

She also knew that Lydia's marriage meant that Wickham was now part of the Bennet

"What Fun!"

family. Would Mr. Darcy ever propose to her again, knowing that a man he hated was to be his wife's brother-in-law?

It was awful, thought Elizabeth. "What would he think if he knew that the proposal I turned down four months ago, I would now so gratefully accept!" She now knew that he was the right man for her. Her understanding and temperment, his talents and compassion, would have been an ideal match. How happy they might have been!

But thoughts of Lydia finally pushed Mr. Darcy out of her mind. Wickham and her sister were finally married and a day later, they arrived in Longbourn. Her mother stepped forward to embrace her runaway daughter. Mr. Bennet was much less cordial.

"Good gracious. What fun this has been! Who knew I would return home married?" Lydia laughed.

Her insensitivity upset Jane, Elizabeth and their father. They studied Wickham carefully.

His affection for Lydia was not equal to hers for him. Their elopement was the result of Lydia's passion, not his. Yet both sisters wanted to hear details of her wedding.

"I was worried that we would never get to the church on time. Uncle had business to settle on me. But I needn't have worried. Mr. Darcy was there to give me away if necessary," Lydia confessed.

"Mr. Darcy!" cried Elizabeth.

"I can't say more. I promised Wickham."

Nothing more was said, but Elizabeth could only guess that Mr. Darcy had acted nobly on her sister's behalf. She could not stand the suspense any longer and wrote to her aunt, begging for an answer.

Elizabeth did not have to wait long for her reply. Her aunt explained that Darcy had come to visit them, because he felt somewhat responsible for Wickham. He blamed his own pride for not informing others of Wickham's worthlessness. He had found out where Lydia

"I Can't Say More."

was. He could not convince her to leave Wickham, so he convinced Wickham to marry her!

"I must also confide, in total secrecy, that it is *Darcy* who is paying Wickham's debts and giving another thousand pounds to Lydia, in addition to what your father has given her. I can only say that both your uncle and I respect and admire him very much!" she concluded.

The letter threw Elizabeth into a highly emotional state. She was amazed that he had done all this. That he had paid for the man he had most wished to avoid. He had done all this for her!

"We owe everything to him," Elizabeth spoke aloud to herself. "Oh, how I regret every unkindness I've ever showed him." She was proud of him, and proud that he had loved her, even though that love was now probably lost forever.

CHAPTER 21

A Dream Fulfilled

The day of Lydia and Wickham's departure soon came. No one, except Mrs. Bennet, was sorry to see them go. Happily, Mrs. Bennet had something else to think about. She heard news that Mr. Bingley was shortly to return to Netherfield!

Jane had also heard of his coming and quickly blushed, though she was quick to add, "The news does not affect me one way or the other." Elizabeth did not know what to make of

She Saw Him Ride Toward the House.

this. Was her sister still hiding her true feelings? She thought that Bingley was still in love with Jane.

"As soon as Mr. Bingley comes, my dear," said Mrs. Bennet to her husband, "you will go to visit him. In any event, I will invite him to dine with us."

So anxious was Mrs. Bennet to send an invitation, that she counted the days until it could be done. Then, on the third morning after Bingley's arrival, she saw him ride towards the house!

Jane kept her place at the table, but Elizabeth went to the window. And what a surprise she got! Mr. Darcy was with Mr. Bingley! Both sisters looked at each other in amazement. What could this mean?

Mrs. Bennet received Mr. Bingley with a great deal of civility, but she barely paid attention to Mr. Darcy at all. She was too busy filling Mr. Bingley in on the news of the neighborhood, even telling him about Lydia's recent marriage as if it had not been anything of a problem!

Elizabeth sat quietly and watched everything. She noted with pleasure how Bingley looked at Jane. He clearly found her as beautiful as ever and spoke to her eagerly. Elizabeth and Darcy, who was not seated next to her, spoke very little. But they could not help glancing at each other frequently.

When the gentlemen rose to go, Mrs. Bennet invited them both to dine at Longbourn in a few days' time.

As soon as they left, Elizabeth went for a walk by herself in order to think. Mr. Darcy's behavior astonished and confused her. "Why did he come if only to be silent? Why didn't he speak to me? What if he no longer cares for me?" she worried.

She didn't have long to ponder these questions. On Tuesday, the dinner party assembled. Bingley quickly seated himself next to Jane. He was very attentive to her all throughout

Glancing at Each Other

dinner. Elizabeth believed that if it were left to him, he and Jane would eventually be married.

Sadly, Mr. Darcy was as far from Elizabeth as was physically possible. In fact, he was seated next to her mother, a situation that could please neither of them. Her mother's manner to him, coupled with the sense of all they owed him, upset Elizabeth deeply. She would have given anything in the world to be able to thank him for all the kindness he had showed Lydia.

Instead, she followed him with her eyes. Darcy walked to another part of the room. She envied everyone he spoke to. "How could I ever be foolish enough to expect a renewal of his love for me? What man would ever propose to a woman a second time?"

She was pleased, though, to bring him coffee and seize the moment to speak to him. "Is your sister still at Pemberley?" she asked softly.

"Yes, till Christmas," he replied. She could think of no more to say, and unfortunately neither could he.

At last, after a young woman whispered something to Elizabeth, he walked away. Then her mother proposed they all play cards, and Elizabeth's spirits dropped. There was no chance of speaking to him now!

Mrs. Bennet did not care about anything now except the future prospects of her eldest daughter. She had seen enough of Bingley's behavior to feel convinced that Jane would finally be his bride.

A few days after this visit, Mr. Bingley called again at Longbourn. He was alone. Mr. Darcy had left that morning for London. "Make haste, Jane," advised her mother, "Mr. Bingley is here."

At first, all the Bennets, except Mr. Bennet who had fled to the library, were in the drawing room. It took some time before Elizabeth was able to move everyone from the room and leave Jane and Bingley alone. When she returned, she saw Bingley and her sister

"I Am So Happy."

PRIDE AND PREJUDICE

together at the hearth, engaged in earnest conversation.

Elizabeth turned to go when Bingley suddenly rose, whispered a few words to Jane, and ran out of the room. "Oh, Lizzy. I am so happy. I must tell mother instantly. Mr. Bingley has gone to speak to father," Jane declared.

Elizabeth, left to herself, smiled. She was delighted that her sister's love affair was well settled at last. All the previous months of suspense and unhappiness were over. In a few minutes, she was joined by Bingley, whose talk with her father had been short and purposeful.

"Where is Jane?" he asked hastily.

"Upstairs, with my mother," Elizabeth smiled. He immediately came to her, claiming the good wishes and affection of a sister. Elizabeth expressed her great pleasure at their coming marriage. They shook hands with great affection.

Indeed, it was a happy day for all in the Bennet household. "Jane, I am very happy for you," announced her father. "You are both ideally suited for one another." Mrs. Bennet, who thought Bingley the handsomest man ever, was forever exclaiming over his wealth and position.

Bingley, from this time on, was a daily visitor at Longbourn. He frequently came before breakfast and always remaining until after supper. Jane was happy that all the truth was finally known.

"Did you know, Lizzy, he told me when he left last November, he really loved me. Nothing would have persuaded him to leave except he thought I was indifferent. I'm glad that he now knows how much I love him!"

Forever Exclaiming Over His Wealth

CHAPTER 22

Lady Catherine's Threats

About a week after Bingley's engagement to Jane had been announced, the Bennet family received an unexpected visitor. A carriage pulled up and the door was thrown open. It was Lady Catherine de Bourgh! She entered with an ungracious air and sat down without saying a word. Elizabeth mentioned her name to her mother when she entered, though no formal introduction took place.

"I hope you are well, Miss Bennet," sniffed

her ladyship. Elizabeth replied that she was.

Mrs. Bennet, with great politeness, asked if her ladyship would care for some refreshment. Lady Catherine refused, but stood and asked, "Miss Bennet, would you care to walk with me?"

Elizabeth agreed and the two began strolling through the grounds of Longbourn. "You must know why I've come," began her ladyship.

Elizabeth looked astonished. "I do not."

"Miss Bennet, an alarming report has reached me. Your own heart, your own conscience, must tell you why I've come."

"I have no idea, madam."

"Don't trifle with me! I was told just two days ago that not only was your sister on the point of entering into an advantageous marriage, but that you, Miss Elizabeth Bennet, would soon marry my nephew, Mr. Darcy. I know this must be a scandalous falsehood, so I insist that you deny this report at once!"

"I haven't heard of any such report," replied

"This Is Outrageous, Miss Bennet!"

Elizabeth.

"Can you declare that there is no foundation for it?" Lady Catherine demanded.

"I do not pretend to possess the same open ways as your ladyship. You may ask all the questions you like, but I may choose not to answer," Elizabeth declared.

"This is outrageous, Miss Bennet!" she cried. "Has my nephew proposed to you? I am entitled to know all his important concerns."

"But you are not entitled to know *mine*," Elizabeth couldn't help answering.

"Be clear. This match can never take place. Mr. Darcy is engaged to my daughter," her ladyship exclaimed. "Now what do you have to say for yourself?"

"Only this. If what you say is so, then why do you ask if he has made an offer to me?" Elizabeth smiled.

"The engagement is of a peculiar kind. My sister, his mother, and I arranged it in infancy. While in their cradles, we planned the union.

Now, at the moment when the wishes of both sisters would be fulfilled by their marriage, you try to prevent it! I won't have my wishes stymied by a woman of inferior birth, with no family of importance in the world."

"What is that to me? You and his mother may have *planned* a marriage. But whether it takes place depends on others. It is up to Mr. Darcy to choose his wife. If Mr. Darcy is neither by honor or inclination interested in marrying his cousin, why is he not free to make another choice? If he chooses me, why can't I accept him?" Elizabeth asked.

"Because honor and decorum forbid it. You will be despised by everyone connected with him. He will lose his friends. Your alliance will be a disgrace."

"Those are heavy misfortunes," agreed Elizabeth. "But the wife of Mr. Darcy will have such an extraordinary source of happiness that, on balance, she will have no regret."

"Headstrong girl! I am ashamed of you. Is

"What Is That to Me?"

this your gratitude to me after the attentions I showered on you last spring? I am not in the habit of being disappointed," bellowed her ladyship.

"That is unfortunate for you. But it has no effect on me," Elizabeth said gently.

"Let me make myself clear. My daughter and my nephew are meant for each other. They are descended on the same noble line on the maternal side. On the father's, they are an ancient, though untitled family. Their fortune on both sides is splendid."

"In marrying your nephew, I don't think I am endangering anyone," Elizabeth insisted. "He is a gentleman. I am a gentleman's daughter. In that, we are equal!"

"True. You are a gentleman's daughter. But who is your mother? Who are your aunts and uncles?"

"Whoever my connections are," said Elizabeth, "if your nephew does not object to them, then why should you?"

"Tell me once and for all, are you engaged to him?"

"I am not."

Lady Catherine seemed pleased. "Will you promise me never to enter into such an engagement?"

"I will make no such promise!" cried Elizabeth heartily. "I will not be intimidated by you. Even if I refuse him, that doesn't mean he will marry your daughter. Your arguments, your ladyship, are ill-judged and frivolous."

"I have one more thing to say," her ladyship nearly screamed with rage. "I know all about your sister's elopement. Is *such* a girl to be my nephew's sister? Is her husband, the son of his late father's butler, to be his brother? Heaven forbid! Are the shades of Pemberley to be so polluted?"

"You have insulted me in every way! I must return home," Elizabeth exclaimed.

"This is your final resolve? You have no regard for the honor of my nephew. Do you not

"An End to Such an Outrage!"

realize that a connection with you will disgrace him in the eyes of society?" She paused. "Are you resolved to have him?"

"I am only resolved to act in a manner which will make me happy, regardless of your feelings," Elizabeth said.

"You are determined to ruin him in the eyes of the world!" Lady Catherine claimed.

"No principle of duty or honor would be violated by my marriage to Mr. Darcy."

"Do not imagine, Miss Bennet, that your ambition will ever be gratified. I came here hoping to find you reasonable. But rest assured, I will not stop until I put an end to such an outrage!" said her ladyship, hastily departing in search of her carriage.

Elizabeth was struck by the heated conversation. She soon learned that Lady Catherine had made the journey from Rosings *solely* to break off her possible engagement to Mr. Darcy! How would he feel about such interference? Would he agree with her? Or would he remain true to his heart? And was his heart still Elizabeth's own? Her own heart was full of doubts. If he doesn't return to Netherfield shortly to visit Bingley, I will know that all is lost.

Elizabeth's thoughts were interrupted by her father, who asked to see her in the library. He told her that Mr. Collins had written him a letter.

"What could he have said?" she asked, as color rose to her cheeks.

"He writes that you will soon be the wife of, in his words, 'one of the most illustrious personages in this land.' Can you guess who is meant by this, Lizzy? It's Mr. Darcy. And Collins warns that Lady Catherine de Bourgh does not view the match with a friendly eye. Mr. Darcy, who never looks at any woman without seeing a blemish and who probably has never looked at you in his life! It is too funny!"

Elizabeth tried to join in her father's amuse-

"It Is His Duty to Warn Us."

ment, but could only force a reluctant smile. Never in the past had his wit been directed so pointedly at her.

"Collins goes on to tell me that it is his duty to warn us that it is unwise for you to rush into a union that is not properly sanctioned. Ha!" he laughed. "What an odious man. There's more. Listen to what he has written:

'I am truly glad that Lydia's sad business has been hushed up. I am only concerned that their living together before the marriage took place should be so generally known. I must not neglect the duties of my station to say that I am amazed that you received the young couple into your house as soon as they were married. You are encouraging vice. You must forgive them as a Christian, but you should never admit them in your sight or allow their names to be mentioned in your hearing.'

"That's his notion of Christian forgiveness, Lizzy! I must say, as much as I hate the hypocrisy of Wickham, Collins is in a class by himself. I cannot wait to write back."

Mr. Bennet re-read the letter with a smile of amusement. "How silly he is, Lizzy. Mr. Darcy is indifferent to you, you dislike him immensely. It is delightfully absurd."

Elizabeth only smiled. How could she tell her father her true feelings? Or how much had changed since they had first met Darcy? Thinking it all over as she sat with Mr. Collins' silly letter in hand, she could scarcely believe it herself.

Yet Darcy had told her, and shown her in so many ways, that he did love her, and her own heart told her that she loved him, too.

"Mr. Darcy, I Must Thank You."

CHAPTER 23

Happy Endings

The next day, Mr. Bingley and Mr. Darcy came to Longbourn. Mrs. Bennet suggested a walk for the foursome. Bingley and Jane lagged behind, eager to be alone. When Elizabeth and Darcy had rounded the corner, out of hearing of the others, she spoke.

"Mr. Darcy, I must thank you for your kindness to Lydia. I have been anxious to tell you how grateful I am. I thank you on behalf of myself and my family."

"Thank me only for yourself," he replied. "I thought only of you."

Elizabeth was too embarrassed to reply. After a short pause, Darcy added, "You must know that my feelings for you are just the same as before. Have you changed your mind about me? Will you marry me? I love you very much!"

"Yes, I have changed my mind about you. I think we could be very happy together. And yes, I want so much to marry you!"

The happiness her reply produced in Darcy was wonderful. He spent the next few moments telling her how delighted he was. She soon learned that his aunt had spoken to him about how stubborn Elizabeth had been.

"It taught me to hope," he said. "I thought I might still have a chance with you."

"We have both changed," she smiled. "We are both more kind, more understanding of each other."

"You know," he nodded, "I was tortured by

"It Taught Me to Hope."

how you refused me last spring. At first, I was angry. Then I realized that you were right about me. That's why I wrote you that letter. Did it make you think better of me?"

"It did. It helped remove my prejudice about you. But please don't torture yourself any longer," she said. "Think only of past memories that give you pleasure."

"I wish I was more like you. I have been selfish all my life," he admitted. "My parents taught me what was right, but I followed those principles only in my pride. I was spoiled and cared for no one beyond my family circle, and to think less of others. I might still be like that if it wasn't for you."

"I knew you were different from the moment I saw you at Pemberley. Did you speak to Mr. Bingley? Is that why he rushed to see Jane?"

"I did. As soon as I realized how much in love she was, I made good my past mistake. You know the rest." They talked and laughed until they reached the house. In the hall, they parted. That night, she told Jane everything.

"But I thought you disliked Mr. Darcy!" Jane exclaimed. Then Elizabeth explained how she gradually came to appreciate all the good qualities in Mr. Darcy. She told Jane how deep and strong her love was for him.

Jane was delighted with Elizabeth's happiness. "I am proud to call him my brother," she said.

The two talked long into the night, wondering how their parents, who disliked Darcy, would take the news of their engagement. Indeed, the very next evening, Darcy sought a private meeting with Mr. Bennet. He emerged after a few minutes with a smile on his face.

"He wants to see you," he whispered to Elizabeth, who was sitting nervously at the table.

She hurried to meet her father, who was stunned by the news. "Lizzy, what are you doing? Are you out of your mind? I thought you have always hated this man!"

Elizabeth was quick to reassure her beloved

"So Darcy Did All That."

father that her attachment to Mr. Darcy was deep and real.

"Or do you mean you are determined to have him? He is rich, to be sure. But will he make you happy? We all know him to be a proud, unpleasant sort of person. But if you truly like him, that changes everything."

"I do, I do like him," she replied with tears in her eyes. "I love him. He has no improper pride. You do not know what he is really like." She went on, in earnest, explaining the gradual change that had occurred. To complete the favorable impression she made, she told her father all that Mr. Darcy had voluntarily done for Lydia.

"This is an evening of wonders! So Darcy did all that. Made up the match, gave the money, paid the fellow's debts and got him his commission! So much the better. It will save me a world of trouble. I would have had to repay your uncle. Now, I'll offer to repay him, and he'll refuse, content to rant on about his love

for you!" her father grinned, his eyes twin-
kling.

"I had no idea!" he continued. "He is a good,
honorable man. In that case, he deserves you.
I could not have parted with you to anyone less
worthy. But I have no idea how your mother
will receive the news," he said, throwing up his
hands.

Elizabeth hoped for the best. When her
mother went to her bedroom, her daughter followed.

"Darcy has asked me to marry him and I
have accepted," she blurted out quickly. Mrs.
Bennet sat down, unable to utter a syllable.
Her daughter feared the worse. Then her
mother exploded in joy.

"Lord bless me! Mr. Darcy! How rich and
great you will be, Lizzy! What jewels! What
carriages!"

That was all Elizabeth needed to hear. Her
spirits rose. Luckily, Mrs. Bennet stood in awe
of her intended son-in-law, so she did not even

"What Jewels! What Carriages!"

venture to speak to him. She treated him with respect and held her tongue. Mr. Bennet made great efforts to get to know Darcy, and Elizabeth was delighted with their friendliness.

Until the wedding, Darcy was a daily visitor at Longbourn. They sat for hours discussing their unusual courtship and how they had come to realize how much they loved each other. The lovers discussed, in great detail, every conversation they had ever had.

"How did you ever fall in love with me? Did you admire my spirit?" Elizabeth asked him playfully one day.

"I admired the liveliness of your mind," Darcy admitted.

"Tell the truth," she laughed. "You were disgusted with the women who were always agreeing with your opinion. I interested you because I was so unlike them." The two went on like that for hours, totally absorbed in each other. All the months of hostility and anger were forgotten in their newfound devotion.

In a few weeks' time, the Bennets had ample cause for celebration. Their two eldest daughters, Jane and Elizabeth, were married. Mrs. Bennet's most fervent wish—to see her daughters married to men of wealth and high social standing—was realized.

Elizabeth moved to Derbyshire to become mistress of Pemberley, Darcy's elegant country estate. Mr. Bennet missed his daughter tremendously. He often went to Pemberley, especially when least expected.

Mr. Bingley and Jane remained at Netherfield for a year, then decided that they were too close to her mother. Even Bingley's easy disposition and Jane's kind heart could not cope with Mrs. Bennet's constant interference. Instead, he bought an estate near Derbyshire, so Jane and Elizabeth could visit regularly.

Pemberley was also the home of Georgiana, Darcy's sister. And the attachment between her and Elizabeth was strong. The young girl was often amazed at how her sister-in-law

They Became the Very Best of Friends.

spoke to her brother. Elizabeth was lively and confident in her own opinions. She gently helped Georgiana to realize that a woman may express herself freely with her husband, when their opinion is grounded in love and respect.

The two young women became the very best of friends. Georgiana had lived a very quiet life, with few friends of her own, her usual companion the governess who accompanied her everywhere. There was no great difference in age between the two sisters-in-law, and the one was eager to learn as the other was to teach.

For Elizabeth, having Georgiana at Pemberley made up for being so far from her own younger sisters. And, she had to admit to herself, Georgiana was a great deal easier to handle than her flighty sisters had ever been. Elizabeth knew, that in observing her marriage to Darcy, the younger woman was learning how good the right marriage could be for both partners.

Elizabeth hoped that when the time came, Georgiana would choose the right man, and for the right reasons. She knew she could best guide her by providing the proper example herself. No, not by myself, Elizabeth corrected herself gently, and with a smile, by our example, Darcy's and mine.

"It's just as I had hoped it would be," Elizabeth told Darcy one night, as they sat together at Pemberley in front of a roaring fire. "I know we shall be happy forever," she said, kissing him softly on the cheek. "We are a true marriage of hearts and minds."

"It's Just as I Hoped."